The Venetians

Short Stories from
La Serenissima

Edward Robert Raupp

Blue Impala Press

THE VENETIANS:
SHORT STORIES FROM *LA SERENISSIMA*

Edward R. Raupp, Ph.D., Lit.D., D.Hon.
10 Hillside Road
North Hampton, New Hampshire 03862
United States of America

Telephone: (603) 502-8864
Email: edraupp@gmail.com
Skype: edward.raupp
Facebook: Edward Raupp
Personal web site: http://sites.google.com/site/edraupp

Printed in the United States of America.
The typeface throughout is Garamond.

Published by Blue Impala Press
North Hampton, New Hampshire 03862
United States of America

ISBN-13: 978-1547268740
ISBN-10: 1547268743

For Danna

Contents

Preface

No city inspires more creativity than does Venice. Painters see in the buildings, canals, and bridges what cannot be seen anywhere else in the world: The Campanile and Basilica of San Marco, the Grand Canal, the Bridge of Sighs, and, of course, the stunning Rialto Bridge, rendered so beautifully on the cover of this book by Filip Mihail. Writers of poetry, novels, and screenplays struggle to avoid the hyperbole that could easily overwhelm the work: from Byron's *Ode on Venice* and Thomas Mann's *Death in Venice*, to Shakespeare's *The Merchant of Venice* and Ian Fleming's James Bond adventure fantasy, *Moonraker*.

And then there is the music. Antonio Vivaldi, virtuoso violinist and one of the leading Baroque composers, was born in Venice, was ordained as a priest, and spent most of his adult life serving the *Ospedale della Pietà* in Venice. Vivaldi's *Four Seasons* may well be the most frequently performed score from the Baroque era. It is those four concerti, with their twelve movements, that inspired and gave structure to this collection of original short stories.

Each concerto has, in turn, an allegro movement, a largo or adagio movement, and a concluding allegro or presto movement. This collection follows the same pattern. Each of the four parts is a season, and each has three short stories. I have tried to follow the Vivaldi pattern: A brisk first story, a more languid or relaxed middle story, and a fast-paced third story, each connected to a Vivaldi sonnet. If the execution of that strategy falls short, I offer my apologies.

PART I. Spring

On the Steps of the Rialto Bridge

Ponte di Rialto

Thursday, May 31, 1945

Springtime is upon us.
The birds celebrate her return with festive song,
    and murmuring streams are softly caressed by the breezes.
Thunderstorms, those heralds of Spring, roar,
    casting their dark mantle over heaven,
Then they die away to silence,
    and the birds take up their charming songs once more.
                        —Antonio Vivaldi, *La Primavera, Allegro*

"You don't understand," Serafina said.

"I'm trying to understand," Ben said, as he raced up the steps of the bridge.

The stroll from the *Palazzo Palladio* along the San Marco side of the Grand Canal was painful for Fina, but she managed with her walking stick. Climbing the steps of the Rialto Bridge was another matter. It was one step at a time.

"No, you're not," she said. "And slow down. Listen to me. You're not trying to understand. You're trying to solve a problem. That's what you do, Ben. I love you. You saved my life, and I'll always be grateful to you, but for you, everything's a problem, and you want to solve it. This isn't just a problem you can solve with algebra. This isn't mathematics, Benjy. It's not an engineering problem."

He stopped and turned back toward her. The morning sun shone on her face, a face that never failed to excite him. High cheekbones. Big brown eyes. Full lips. "Well, we *do* have a problem, Fina. The war's over. We won. Hitler's dead. The Germans have all surrendered. Mussolini's dead and gone, along with his Fascism. The Italian Campaign is finished. Now the division's preparing to move east to Trieste in two weeks. They're rushing to pack up. The OSS is disbanding, and the division commander wants me to join his staff. I'd say that presents a problem."

She took his hand. Partly to steady herself on the steps, but mostly because she loved his touch. From the first time he touched her, when he lifted her and carried her to the medics, she felt safe with him. More than safe. Warm. Loved.

She took a deep breath and sighed. "The partisans are leaving, too. Some from our band have already gone to Trieste. What a crazy world! We fight Mussolini's Fascists. Then we fight Hitler's Nazis. Now we run to fight Tito's Communists. It just keeps going on and on. Now you're going to Trieste, too. You're leaving me."

"I'll come back, Fina. It's not far. I'll resign my commission. They don't need me now. They'll be happy to get rid of me. I'm sure the OSS will be scrapped. I'll come back as fast as I can. I'll be a civilian again. I'll come back."

"Will you, Ben? Will you come back to me? Will you come back to Venice?"

"You know I will. I don't ever want to be separated from you. Meeting you is the best thing that has ever happened to me. We'll get married when I return."

2

"In the church?" she asked. "Do you want to get married in the church? In the *Chiesa di San Bartolomeo?*"

"You know that's not possible."

"It's possible. If you convert."

"We've talked about that, Fina. Why can't we just have a civil ceremony?"

"No priest? Of course, it's all right with me. Anyway, it's been a long time since I've been at the church. So much has happened during the war, and under Mussolini. Where was God? Where was God when all those people were being tortured and killed? But still, it's a tradition."

"We don't need that kind of tradition. We don't need a priest. The Mayor can do it. In the *Palazzo Cavalli*. When I get back, we'll go to the Registry Office and get a license. The Mayor knows us. He'll do it. Problem solved, Fina. We'll be just as married in the *Palazzo Cavalli* as in the *Chiesa di San Bartolomeo*." He stopped on the step next to Serafina and kissed her on the cheek.

"Oh, Ben!" she said, taking his hand. "You still don't understand. There's Mamma."

"Mamma Rose," he said. "She likes me, Fina. She calls me *mio figlio*. She's always pinching my cheek. She really does like me."

Fina laughed. "She does, Ben. She really likes you. She thinks we're a good match. Is she right?"

"I'm sure she's right. I think we were a good match from the moment we met, that moment when I found you in the forest. I hate that you were so badly hurt, but if that hadn't happened, we might never have met."

"It was a small price I paid, getting shot. I like the way you tell the story."

Serafina Palladio was always an eager listener when Ben told her his story. And she wanted to know more about this young American who had saved her life. She learned that when Ben graduated from Carnegie Tech on June 10, 1942, he was commissioned second lieutenant in the United States Army's Corps of Engineers. He expected to get into the action as a platoon leader in an engineer battalion in one of the Army's recently activated infantry divisions. Instead he was immediately assigned to the Army's newly formed Office of Strategic Services, the OSS, and, after just two weeks of training at Fort Benning, Georgia, he was flown to England, and from there, he parachuted behind the German lines in Italy to meet up with the partisans.

It was an assignment that would change the life of this teenaged girl from Venice. She would always be grateful to the American Army for sending Ben to Italy. For assigning him to work with the partisans. It was more than pure chance that he happened to be in her area of operations when she felt that searing pain in her leg. If she believed in miracles, this would qualify.

Ben wasn't shy. When Fina would press him to tell her more about his life up to the moment they met, he would tell her about his letters in football, baseball, basketball, and track. He told her that his major in civil engineering, with minors in the German and Italian languages, along with his high school semester in Rome in the fall of 1936, all made him an ideal candidate for the kind of mission OSS had in mind. He knew how to build bridges, and he knew how to blow them up.

Official Army records showed that a Captain Benjamin Aaron Tomlinson was assigned to the G2 Intelligence Section of the 88th Infantry Division, but Ben seldom appeared anywhere near the division headquarters. Instead, he was in the field, keeping in close contact with the partisans. It seemed to Fina that Ben's area of operations, his AO, was large, much larger than her own. Her team of partisans moved swiftly from one point to another, like the hunter-gatherers of pre-historic times. Ben coordinated not only with her band but with others from Vicenza in the north to Ravenna in the south, from Bologna in the west to the east coast of the Adriatic Sea.

After four months of bitter fighting around Monte Cassino, ninety miles southeast of Rome, the 88th Division continued to push the Germans north, battle after battle, until it reached a point just south of Padua in the spring of 1944. Ben and his partisan band moved north ahead of the Division, gathering intelligence on the German units and conducting sabotage operations on their supply points, especially their fuel stations.

It was there, after a skirmish with a German patrol, that he found Fina in a wooded area, bleeding from the bullet that had shattered her left leg and torn through an artery. He tied off the wound and ran, carrying her in his arms, nearly two miles farther south to the 313th Medical Battalion aid station. After she was stabilized, an ambulance took them to the 11th Field Hospital six miles to the south.

Ben held her hand in the ambulance and all the way to the operating room. He stayed at her bedside after the surgery. When she recovered from the anesthesia and opened her eyes, the first face she saw was Ben's.

"Good morning," he said. "You're going to be all right." He told her how he had found her, how he stopped the bleeding, and how he had gotten her to the hospital. "But I don't know your name. I'm Ben. Benjamin Tomlinson, Captain, United States Army." She smiled and squeezed his hand before she went back to sleep. It would be another day before he learned *her* name.

"Serafina," she said. "My name is Serafina Palladio. From Venice. Thank you for saving my life. *Grazie molto.*"

"It's not every day I have the chance to save the life of a beautiful young partisan," Ben said.

"You have been here by my bedside all this time?"

"Except for when you were in surgery. That's when I had a chance to shower and shave. I think I was rather dirty when we got here, Miss Palladio."

"My friends call me Fina," she said. "I think we must be friends? No?"

After two weeks, Fina was still mending, but she was impatient to get back into action. Dismissing the advice of the surgeon, she left the hospital as soon as she could manage, with a walking stick in her right hand and holding on to Ben with her left hand.

Along with other bands of partisans, Fina and Ben fought the Germans together over the following year. They sent intelligence reports back to the Italian Committee for National Liberation, to the 88th Division Headquarters, and to the Special Operations Executive, Britain's counterpart to the American OSS. Fina walked slowly and took cover behind large rocks, but she was an expert sharpshooter with a steady hand and was able to pick off a dozen German officers with her 7.52 mm Carcano carbine.

Neither Ben nor Fina can tell with much precision exactly when they fell in love. Ben will say it was love at first sight. Fina will say it just grew from gratitude to love somewhere in the forests. When the Germans surrendered at the end of April 1945, Fina invited Ben to travel with her to her home in Venice.

"She likes that you bring her chocolates."
"And me."
"And you. All the young men were gone from the city. She was happy to see a young man. And you look Italian. A little."

Ben's ancestry is mixed enough so there might well be some Italian. There's a bit of Eastern European Ashkenazi on his father's side, a bit of Nordic from his German mother's side, and a few other bits lost to time. His hair is dark, but not black like Serafina's, which had grown longer since the injury that had slowed, but not stopped, her active operations. His hair, too, had grown longer than Army regulations prescribed, but in his line of work, there was no one to argue the point.

"She's a wonderful cook," he said. "It's amazing what she can do with pasta."

"Maybe someday we'll have meat. Then you'll have a feast like you've never had in your life."

"I'll bring some beef from the mess hall. Or lamb."
"And pork?"

"And pork," he said with a smile. Ben's family had never kept kosher, to the great disappointment of his father's parents. And as for the rites of passage, he had undergone neither *bar mitzvah* nor confirmation.

She took his hand as they climbed the steps to the top of the bridge. She stumbled once, but Ben caught her. She looked at him and smiled.

As a girl, Serafina Palladio would race up those steps with her friends. She had the longest legs and would always win. There would be no more racing. Each step was now agony.

"When we get married, we'll go to my home in Brooklyn," Ben said. "My family has money. They know the best doctors. They'll fix your leg."

"Brooklyn?"

"It's part of New York City. Many Italians live there. You'll make lots of friends."

"Brooklyn America," she said, wrinkling her brow. "I know Brooklyn. Many Italian families have moved to that place. I'm sure it's a nice place. Maybe the streets are paved with gold. Maybe not. But this is my *home*, Benjy. Venice. *Venezia*. I can't leave this place. My family's been here for five hundred years. Maybe a thousand. Maybe more. This is my bridge, Benjy. This is my canal. Look at it. Those are my gondolas on the Grand Canal. Those are my gulls flying all around. So, now I walk with a limp. Is that *importante* to you, Signor Beniamino Tomlinson? That I walk with a limp and can hardly manage to climb the steps of the Rialto Bridge? Maybe you'll be ashamed of such a cripple for a wife. Walking down the street in Brooklyn USA with a cripple?"

"Fina, don't you know me better than that by now? What's important to me is that you're well. It's important to me that you're happy. I love you, Fina. I'm upside down in love with you, and I want to spend the rest of my life making you happy. Is that so bad? Wanting to make you happy?"

Each step was painful for Fina, but she was determined to make it to the top of the bridge. She kept climbing, one step at a time, holding his hand with a tight grip. "I can do this, Ben," she said, wincing. "I've climbed these steps a thousand times. I can do it."

She shivered as she recalled the sharp pain when the bullet tore into her leg. Even though she was in shock, she recalled dimly seeing Ben when he found her lying in a pool of blood. She could never forget the pain. She could never forget feeling so helpless. She passed in and out of consciousness.

She recalled his carrying her to the aid station. She was so light, so thin from being on the run for many months with the partisans from Veneto and Padua. Of all the missions she had been on, this is the one she would remember most, the one she could never forget. How could she forget the one mission that would change her life forever? She remembered Ben pinning his own Purple Heart medal on her gown while she was lying on the cot in the hospital. She remembered his kiss on her cheek.

"I love you, too, Ben. Maybe more than you know. It's not just gratitude. I've seen how you treat people. With respect. With dignity. You didn't know who I was in the forest. But you took care of me. You saved my life. You love people. You respect everyone. Even the prisoners we took in the mountains. I remember thinking, I could love a man like that. Mamma doesn't call you her son because you bring her chocolates. She's seen so much these past years. She knows how to judge someone. She wants a son. Not just any son. She wants you to be her son, Benjy. Her real son."

"We'll have a real Italian wedding celebration for Mamma," Ben said. "Right here on the bridge. *Your* bridge, Fina. We'll invite everybody. We'll have spaghetti and ravioli and lasagna with meat. We'll have lots of fruits and nuts and vegetables and the biggest wedding cake Venice has ever seen! Then we can have our honeymoon in New York. You'll have your leg fixed. Then we'll come back. We'll live here. In Venice."

Fina smiled and squeezed Ben's hand. "On the Grand Canal, Benjy?" she asked. "In the Palazzo Palladio? Mamma would like that. With a nice view of the Rialto Bridge?"

"On the Grand Canal," he said. "In the Palazzo Palladio. With a *glorious* view of the Rialto Bridge."

With that, he picked her up and raced up the remaining steps to the top of the bridge. "Just look at that, Fina. The Grand Canal. It's there for you and me. Forever!"

She laughed. "I think you understand."

Il Pescheria, The Fish Market

Mercato di Rialto

Saturday, June 16, 1934

On the flower-strewn meadow,
with leafy branches rustling overhead,
the goat-herd sleeps,
his faithful dog beside him.
—Antonio Vivaldi, *La Primavera, Largo*

"You look tired," Gaspare Moretti said to his friend of more than sixty years. Born and raised together in the same Dorsoduro neighborhood near the waterfront of the Giudecca Canal, they were baptized and confirmed together at *Santa Maria della Visitazione,* the Church of the Visitation, on *Zattere,* Dorsoduro's waterfront promenade. Gaspare and Rigo Lucarini had been fishermen on the Lagoon and in the Adriatic Sea all their lives, since they were boys of eight years old. They grew up on the boats, on the water, rowing and casting nets. Hauling big fish out of the water and onto their boat. Now they take the catch from the boats of younger men and sell at *Il Pescheria,* the Rialto fish market, to homemakers and buyers for the many restaurants and hotels in and around the city of Venice.

"I can't keep my eyes open," Rigo Lucarini said. He coughed.

"Still coughing," Gaspare said. "Here, let me feel your forehead." He put his big rough hand on Rigo's forehead. "You're burning up," he said.

11

"I'm all right," Rigo said. "Stop fussing."

"I fuss because you're my friend. My best friend. And you're tired and you're sick."

"Just like my mother, God rest her soul. She was a good woman, a good mother. But she was always fussing. Stop fussing. You're not my mother."

"It's been a long day, my friend. Let's finish cleaning up and go home," Gaspare said. "You'll get a little rest, eh? The rest will be good for you." The smell of the morning's catch was still in the air. Gaspare wiped the top of the wooden counter with a rag that once was a white singlet that had long since served its purpose as clothing for a respectable man.

"How can I rest? All this bad news. All I do is worry. I can't sleep," Rigo said. He took the rag from Gaspare and started to wipe the wooden legs of the counter. The fish smell would never be completely gone, but he tried anyway. He didn't mind the smell, but the women who did the shopping for the hotels held their noses when they came to the fish market if the smell got too strong. So, he wiped.

"You mean this German pipsqueak? This little paperhanger with his funny moustache? What kind of man has such a moustache? If he wants to have a moustache, let him have a *real* moustache, not that funny little thing under his nose." Gaspare made a gesture with his hand and arm, a gesture one would not make in polite company.

"Why do you think I'm worried?" Rigo said. "You think I mean our Primo losing to that German Max Baer in New York City America on Thursday? Or *Il Duce* inviting that other German to Venice?"

"That was terrible," Gaspare said.

"Which one?" Rigo asked. "That little Hitler in the *Piazza San Marco* or Primo Carnera losing in the eleventh round? I don't know which was worse." He coughed again.

"Primo didn't lose. It was robbery," Gaspare said. "It was the big wheels. They couldn't stand to have an Italian World Heavyweight Champion. Prejudice, that's what it was. My cousin Aldo in New York told me there's so much prejudice against Italians in America. That's what it was. Prejudice. You see?"

"It wasn't prejudice," Rigo said. "Let's face it. He was finished. How many times did he hit the canvas? What did they say on the radio? Ten? Twelve times? Primo wasn't ready for that fight. He wasn't ready. He didn't train hard enough. Too much high living. Too many American women. All that money and fame. It went to his head. He didn't take the fight seriously. He embarrassed us."

"The referee should have let them fight," Gaspare said. "That referee, I think he must have been German. They have a lot of Germans in America, you see. A lot of Germans. That referee. He must have been a German. He had no right to call it a technical knockout in the eleventh round. A knockout is a knockout. What's a *technical* knockout, anyway? There's no such thing as 'technical.' It's a knockout or it's not a knockout. Isn't that right, Rigo? It's a knockout or it's not a knockout. Isn't that right?"

"A good boy," Rigo said. "Primo was a good boy. Remember when he was at school over there, in Sequals? He was big even then. Biggest boy in the school. Champion of the world! Imagine! Our Primo. Champion of Italy. World Heavyweight Champion. What? For a year. Not even a year. Anyway, who's talking about Primo Carnera?"

13

"*We* are," Gaspare said. "We're talking about Primo Carnera losing to that German, Max Baer, by a technical knockout in the eleventh round. That's what we're talking about."

"No, no!" Rigo said. "I mean that other German. That new guy they just elected last year. Hitler. Adolf Hitler. What did you call him?"

"Pipsqueak. I said he's a pipsqueak. Not like Benito. Not like *Il Duce*. Not even in his league."

"Maybe," Rigo said. "But he worries me, this Hitler guy." Rigo was always the worrier. He worried about the catch. He worried about the weather. And he's been worrying about Mussolini since 1922.

"You're tired," Gaspare said. "You need some sleep. We'll go to mass tomorrow and pray about all this stuff. The priest will pray for a strong Italy. He'll pray for *Il Duce* and he'll pray for the Army."

"I'm not going to mass tomorrow."

"What?"

"You heard me. I'm not going to mass," Rigo said. "Not going. That's all. How many times have we gone to mass? All our lives. I've paid my dues. And what do we get in return? Words. Empty words."

"What are you talking about?" Gaspare whispered. "What do you mean, you paid your dues?" Absence from Sunday's mass is noticed. Noticed by members of the congregation, and especially by the priest. The priest would be expecting you at Confession on Friday if you missed mass. Missing mass is a serious offense in the Church.

"Not going," Rigo said. "I've had enough. I'm never going to set foot inside that church again as long as I live."

14

"You're talking rubbish," Gaspare said. "Of course, you're going to mass tomorrow. We go to mass every Sunday. We've been going to mass together all our lives. What will people say? The neighbors, Rigo. What will the neighbors say? I'll tell you what they'll say. They'll say, 'Old Rigo and Gaspare. They disrespect the Church. Maybe they don't believe in God.' That's what they'll say. They'll say we're atheists. Or worse. Can you imagine? No, no. We'll go to mass together, just like we always do."

"I'm sorry," Rigo said. "I've been thinking."

"Thinking? When did you start thinking? About what? What are you thinking about? Tell me what you're thinking about and why you're not going to mass tomorrow. Eh? Tell me," Gaspare demanded. "Tell me, Rigo. What are you thinking all of a sudden?"

"The day before yesterday, this Hitler comes to our city. This *animale*. This uncultured pig. This *pazzo*. This madman. He's crazy. I tell you, he's crazy. Even Benito thinks so. He called him 'a mad little clown,' and you know I don't like what Benito has done. Now *Il Duce* invites this 'mad little clown' to *La Serenissima*. It's an insult. That's what it is. An insult to Venice. This pair of crazy corporals."

"Crazy corporals," Gaspare said. "Yes, I suppose that's what they are. Crazy corporals fighting the last war all over again. This time, maybe they'll win, eh?"

"Tyrants. Murderers," Rigo said. "And where are the priests while all this is going on, eh? Are they raising their voices against these madmen? How can I go to mass when the priests babble their hollow words but say nothing about what's really going on? Like Nero. Fiddling while our civilization is burning."

"Rigo, be careful. There are spies everywhere."

"Garbage. *Spazzatura.* Spies. Swine. That's what they are. They're swine. *Sono suina.* You know what we need, eh?"

"Tell me, Rigo. What do we need?"

"We need a republic."

"A republic," Gaspare said. "What republic? What are you talking about?"

"No king," Rigo said. He coughed. "No king. We need to be the Republic of Italy. Like America."

"You want, what? United States of Italy? Rigo, Rigo, did we not learn Italy history in school? In the same year you and I were born, in 1861, we became the Kingdom of Italy. We already have a United States of Italy. No more separate little countries. One country."

"That's just it. *Kingdom* of Italy. Why we need a king? How much fish he has caught, this King, eh? This tiny little man. What has he ever done for the people, eh? Tell me that. With all his fancy uniforms. He said Italian boys would not be killed in the Great War. My first born, Salvatore – you were his godfather – killed in that war. Your son, my godson, Paolo – killed in that war. Where was the tiny little Victor Emmanuel, eh? Was he on the front lines, eh? I say he's a murderer. We don't need such a murderer. We don't need a king to send our boys to die in some stupid war. We need to be rid of the King and have a republic. Government of the people. That's what we need. Not government of rich murderers."

"Slow down, Rigo. Slow down. You'll get into trouble if you keep talking like that. Be careful. They're listening. Mussolini has big ears. Always, they're listening. You want to get us both in trouble, eh?"

"And the Pope," Rigo said. "Where is the Pope while all this is going on? Hiding in his palace in the Vatican." He wiped his watery eyes with his sleeve.

"The Pope? Rigo, quiet. Shh," Gaspare said. "You mustn't…"

"Mustn't? Mustn't what? Think?" He coughed.

"That's the priest's job," Gaspare said. "To think. The priest does the thinking. We do the fishing."

"We *used* to do the fishing," Rigo said. "There was honor in fishing. Bravery. Trust. We trusted each other. Our lives depended on trust. Remember the time our boat turned over. You saved my life. I trusted you. Always."

"You would have done the same for me."

"Now there are spies. Nobody trusts anybody else. Mussolini has spies. Pius has spies. The King has his spies. They all have spies. Get rid of them, I say. All of them. What we need? I tell you what we need. We need another Gaetano Bresci. That's what we need."

Gaetano Bresci assassinated the king's father in the city of Monza on July 29, 1900.

"Careful," Gaspare said. "Talk like that will get us both arrested."

"Once we did the fishing," Rigo said. "Now we are just *pescivendolo*. Now we're just a couple of old men selling the fish that young men catch."

"That's the way of life," Gaspare said. "It was the same for our fathers. And *their* fathers. It will be same for our sons and for our daughters. Our time has come and gone. Their time is now. Then it will be gone. So it goes."

"Ah, Gaspare, my friend. You have become a philosopher. The Marcus Aurelius of Venice."

17

"You don't need to be a philosopher to see how the world works."

"No, but it helps. Oh! I must sit down." He coughed a rasping cough. "Give me a hand, Gaspare. I'm feeling so weak. I can't stand up. I'm dizzy. Everything's spinning."

Gaspare reached behind the wooden counter and brought out a small stool. "Here. Sit."

Rigo lowered himself to sit on the stool.

"I told you," Gaspare said. "I said you look tired. Didn't I say that?" Gaspare held Rigo's arm to help keep his balance.

"Yes. You said that. I have to rest."

"*Sì,*" Gaspare said. "Take a rest. Just sit here for a while. Then we'll go home, eh?"

"Home," Rigo said. "I'd like to go home." Rigo bowed his head. His muscles ached and his cataract-clouded brown eyes were watering; tears ran down his cheeks.

"Just sit for a while. A few minutes, eh?"

Gaspare leaned against a stout wooden post and looked out past the rows of countertops, now all wiped clean from the day's catch. Small boats were passing the market on the Grand Canal toward *Piazza San Marco* on the right, and toward Santa Lucia Train Station on the left.

It was mid-morning and all sorts of watercraft were passing the Fish Market. Gaspare and Rigo had been at the Market since sunrise, hauling fish from the boats that pulled up to the docks. The work may not be as rewarding as being out in the fresh sea air catching tuna, gray mullet, and salmon, and pulling them aboard the boat, but at least they could take a little break now and then, sit down, maybe doze off, and not worry about falling overboard.

"You remember the time we caught that great big blue shark? Over two meters it was," Gaspare said. He laughed. "That was funny, wasn't it? It was so big it hardly fit in the boat. Remember, Rigo? Remember that little boat we had? Remember that day when the waves were more than three meters high? And the wind! It nearly blew our boat out of the water. But we managed to keep it pointed into the wind, and we rode it out. We laughed afterward, but I can tell you, I thought we were going down. Remember, Rigo? I thought we were going down. I thought we were finished. Oh, there were some rough seas in those days. You know something? I'll tell you. I'm glad to be finished with it. Yes, I'm glad. Let the young men bring the fish and we'll sell them here in the market, eh, Rigo. Rigo? Sleeping already? Rigo? Rigo? Oh, Rigo, no!" Gaspare cried. He knelt beside his old friend, held him in his arms, and kissed him on the cheek. "Oh, Rigo."

The Unicorn in *Giardini Papadopoli*

An Island in the Lagoon

Mid-May, A Long, Long Time Ago

Led by the festive sound of rustic bagpipes,
nymphs and shepherds lightly dance
beneath the brilliant canopy of spring.
            —Antonio Vivaldi, *La Primavera, Allegro*

"You're fast but rather small," she said. "I hope you don't mind my saying so."

The smell of jasmine was in the air, and bright purple bougainvillea peeked out from green laurel hedges. A bright yellow bird sat easily on her shoulder.

"It's all right. I don't mind at all," he said, prancing around the hibiscus shrubs, with their bright red flowers. "I'm just a growing boy."

"You're not a boy at all," she said. "I know a boy when I see one, and you are not a boy. In fact, unless I'm mistaken, you're a *horse*. A little horse. With a horn in the middle of his forehead."

"I was speaking figuratively," he said. "Haven't you ever heard of poetic license?"

"Hah! Now I've seen everything. A horse who thinks he's a poet!" The yellow bird flew to a nearby branch.

"I'm learning. My teacher's a great poet. The greatest poet in the world."

"And who might that be, if I may ask? Who do you say is the greatest poet in the world?"

"You may ask," he replied, "and I shall tell you. He's a human everyone calls Homer, but I call him *Dáskalos*, Teacher. He's a great poet and he knows a lot of history."

"Hmm. That sounds like Greek," she said. "I know some Greek language. My people escaped from the Greeks many years ago. Would this greatest poet in the world happen to be a Greek?"

"Of course. What did you think? Did you think I was a barbarian? *Bar, bar, bar?* No, I have the good fortune to have been born in the greatest country in the world. We have arts and science. We have great philosophers and poets. I'm happy to be a Greek."

"My people don't like Greeks," she said. "Especially the Myrmidons, the savages of Achilles. They did terrible things to my ancestors in Troy. You're not a Myrmidon, are you? I wouldn't like to think I was having a conversation with a Myrmidon. My parents wouldn't have approved."

"Your parents?"

"Over there. In that grove of olive trees. That's where their ashes are buried."

"Oh, I'm sorry," he said. "You're an orphan. I didn't know. And, by the way, I'm not a Myrmidon."

"Good. They taught me well. Never forget. And beware of horses. That's what they told me. Never forget what the Greeks did to our homeland."

"That was a long time ago," he said. "Isn't it time to put all that behind?"

"We remember. Our parents told us about the war. Ten years of war. So many of our people killed. We remember. Just because a girl didn't want to be married to an old man and wanted to be with the boy she loved."

"Let me ask you a question. Do you know any Greeks? Have you ever met a real Greek? Not just in old stories, but today?"

"No. Just you. You're the first Greek I've ever met."

"I don't think you have any reason to dislike me."

"Well, my people don't like horses either."

"But I'm not a horse. As you can see."

"I had no idea there were creatures like you."

"Creatures like me, indeed!"

"Well, what are you? I've never seen a horse – excuse me, you do look a lot like a horse – a horse with a horn in the middle of his forehead."

"In my language, I'm called *Monókeros*. In your language, you may call me *Unicorno*."

"Well, you're a most unusual being, *Signor Unicorno*."

"May I take that as a compliment, *Signorina?*"

"You may, *Signor Unicorno*," she replied. "Actually, I think you're kind of cute."

He blushed. The pink of his cheeks shone against the bright white of his head and body.

"If I may return the compliment, *Signorina*, I think you are quite cute yourself…for a human, that is."

It was her turn to blush. She turned away and smiled. "How is it you come to be here, *Signor Unicorno?*" she asked. "What brings you to our little island?"

"Why, you called me," he said.

"I called you? There must be some mistake."

"The gods don't make mistakes. They can be peculiar, sometimes mischievous, but mistakes, never. Well, almost never. I remember the time when Zeus…"

"The gods sent you?" she asked.

22

"Yes. Well, one god. Aphrodite. Are you not Laodice Ponticelli, of the *Venetos* people of the Lagoon?"

"I am Laodice. And yes, my people are *Venetos della Laguna*. Our ancestor is Aeneas, Prince of Troy."

She approached the unicorn tentatively.

"Aeneas, son of that very same Aphrodite, and of Anchises, first cousin to King Priam. My people came from south of here, from the place of Romulus, where there was so much war. They found peace, here, in the lagoon."

"Ah, peace. We all wish for peace. But more. And you, my lovely young Princess of Troy, child of the Aeneans, did you not look at the stars last night and utter a lament?"

"A lament?"

"Did you not cry that you are lonely?" he asked. "Did you not wish for someone to be a companion? Someone to love? Someone who will love you? Was that not you? Did you not ask for someone to love?"

"Yes, I did," she replied, "but a man, not a horse! Sorry. *Unicorno.*"

"Oh," he laughed, "not I! As lovely as you may be – for a human – you are decidedly not my type."

"And as cute as you are," she agreed, "you are definitely not *my* type. So how is it that you came in place of a man?"

"Aphrodite heard your prayer and sent me to carry you to a place where there *is* a young man who *also* asks for a companion, someone to love, someone who will love him."

"A young man?" she asked.

"A young man," he replied, "and not far from here. We can fly there in just a few minutes."

23

"Fly? Ah, I see, you have wings!" she exclaimed. "I hadn't noticed. Do you all have wings? All *unicorno*, I mean."

"No, not all," he said. "Just a chosen few. But I'm happy to have them, so we can fly to meet your young man."

"Must we *fly?*" she asked. "I've never left the land before, except for swimming."

"Flying to the other island is better than swimming, don't you think?"

"I'm a good swimmer," she said.

"Well, you're welcome to try, but flying will be much easier. And faster. I'll carry you on my back."

"And suppose I fall off? I've never been on the back of a horse – sorry – any creature, and I've never flown. Of course, I see the great grey herons on the shores of the lagoon, and they seem to fly without much effort, but they aren't carrying anyone on their backs."

"You won't fall off. Trust me. I promise to make sure you'll be safe. Don't worry. Just hold on to my mane. It will be a smooth ride."

"How can I be sure you'll keep your promise? How do I know you won't drop me into the sea? Maybe Aphrodite just wants to get rid of me. Maybe she's tired of my 'lament.' Maybe she wants to kill me because I'm not Greek. How can I trust you? How can I trust *her*? She *is* Greek, after all. And my people don't trust Greeks, especially after that wooden horse trick in Troy."

"Listen. Aphrodite regrets those ten years of war between Greece and Troy. She didn't want to start a war. She was just trying to make a good match. As you said, two young people in love. That's what it was all about."

"She was just trying to make a match?"

"She didn't think it would get to the point of a thousand ships coming to take the girl back to her old husband. He was an old man, and she was a young girl. Why didn't he just let her go? Aphrodite didn't think he would go crazy and start such a terrible war."

"She didn't know? She's a god. Aren't the gods supposed to know everything? She should have known."

"She always thought there could be a peaceful settlement. And, by the way, I don't think she saw that wooden horse trick coming, either."

Laodice looked up at the white puffy clouds in the powder blue sky. Then she turned to the unicorn. "You're sure she wouldn't try to hurt me?"

"Absolutely! She considers you her own child. Her blood flows in your veins. She would never hurt you. She's a lover, not a killer. Now, Aries, her brother. That's a different story. He's the killer in the family."

"She doesn't kill anyone? With all her power?"

"Aphrodite doesn't kill people – directly. She's the lover in the family. She doesn't like to see people fighting. When she sees a lonely girl on a small island, and a lonely boy on another small island nearby, she takes it on herself to bring the two lovers together. Of course, that thing with Helen and Paris, well, that didn't work out so well."

"Not well at all," she said.

"But most of the time, it comes out right. You should see the smile on her face when a good match is made. Why, just last week…"

"All right, all right. Enough! I'll go with you. I'm not married to some old man, so I won't be the cause of a war. Now, how do I get up on your back?" she asked.

"Here, I'll kneel down. Take hold of my mane and pull yourself up." With that, he knelt so she could climb on his back.

"Won't it hurt? I mean when I pull on your mane?"

"It won't hurt," he said. "Come on! Let's go."

"Wait!" she said. "I don't even know your name. You know my name, but I don't know *your* name. I think I should know the name of one who makes such promises."

"Hermogenes. They call me Hermogenes, born of Hermes. Hermes is the messenger of the gods, and I am also a messenger. Well, actually, I'm just an apprentice messenger. Aphrodite thought it best not to send Hermes. She thought you might fall in love with him. He is most handsome."

"She thought I would fall in love with Hermes? So, she sent *unicorno?*"

"She's thoughtful that way," he said. "Now, let's go. This kneeling is not a comfortable position."

"Wait! You haven't told me anything about this young man who's supposed to be the answer to my lament."

He stood up. "Now, look," he said, with a bit of agitation in his voice. "You need to have faith in the good judgment of the goddess of love. In her matchmaking. She's good at matchmaking. You'll see."

"But is he handsome?" she asked. "Hermogenes, is he handsome?

"Is that what you want?" he asked. "Is he handsome? I don't know if he's as handsome as Hermes or Apollo, or if he's not handsome. Narcissus was handsome. So handsome that he died looking at his own reflection in a pool of water. Is that what you want, a handsome man?"

26

"Well, have you seen him?" she asked.

"No, I have not seen him, but I trust in Aphrodite's judgment. So should you."

"Well, if he's not handsome, maybe he's strong. Or rich. Or tall. Is he strong, or rich, or tall? What do you think?"

"Princess Laodice," he said, "you must have faith in Aphrodite, whose blood you carry. She has a personal interest in you. This will be a good match. She will not disappoint you. Have faith, Princess."

"All right," she said. "I have faith. I've decided. I'll do it. I'll go with you."

"Good," he said, as he knelt again. "Climb aboard."

"Wait! Is he of the *Venetos* people? Is he of the family of our father Aeneas?" she asked.

He sighed. "Such questions! Is that important to you? Is he handsome? Is he strong? Is he rich? Is he tall? Is he of the *Venetos* people?"

"Well, does he speak our language? Does he know our ways?" she asked. "You know, we're a noble people. We have our traditions. Our line goes all the way back to King Priam and Queen Hecuba, to Aeneas and Creusa."

Hermogenes rose again from the uncomfortable kneeling position and started prancing around the showy hibiscus and pawing the ground, eager to get on with his mission.

"The young man Aphrodite has chosen for you lives on the Isle of Ithaca in the Middle Sea. He's also from a noble people. In fact, he's the Prince of Ithaca, descended from King Odysseus. He's Greek, if you must know."

"Greek! Again Greek!" she exclaimed.

"Yes, Greek," he said. "And what's wrong with being Greek?" His eyes became sad. He turned his head away. A tear formed at the corner of his eye.

"Oh! I hurt you," she said. "I'm sorry. I forgot. You're Greek, too. Forgive me. I've always been told not to trust Greeks. From the time I was a child I remember my parents saying, 'Beware of Greeks bearing gifts.' They told stories of how they killed so many of our family in Troy."

She put her arms around the little unicorn's neck and touched his cheek. It was soft and silky. He rested his head on her shoulder.

"It's all right," he said. "I understand. But Greek or Venetos. What's the difference? If you love each other, you'll be happy. What's important to you, Princess Laodice Ponticelli? Handsome? Tall? Kind? Language?"

"No," she replied, "none of those. Except *kind*, of course. I could not love a cruel man."

"I can assure you he will not be cruel," he said. "Aphrodite knows him, and she knows you. Have faith in her judgment, Laodice. If you speak different languages, you will each learn the language of the one you love. Whatever the problem, love is the answer."

"Love is the answer? That sounds like a good philosophy."

"It will get you through the tough times, Princess. Love one another. That's a philosophy that really is worth remembering."

"All right, I agree. I'll go with you. But you must grant me one wish."

"One wish?"

"More like a request," she said.

28

"And what is your wish? Your request?"

"You must bring us back."

"Both of you? Back here to the lagoon?"

"I put my trust in Aphrodite. If she thinks this is a good match, then I agree to the match. But we must start our family here. In this place. This will be the place where a new people will live in peace and love. Promise me."

"I promise. I will bring you both back. Now climb up." He knelt again. She took hold of his mane and lifted herself onto his back and rested her cheek on his soft neck. He spread his wings and, gently but swiftly, rose above the sweet-smelling jasmine, above the herons walking along the shoreline of the lagoon, above the edge of the water, pink-tinted with hundreds of flamingos, and over the tall cypress trees, and headed east, into a rising orange sun.

PART II. Summer

Clouds Over the Lagoon

Riva degli Schiavoni, Canale di San Marco

Saturday, July 19, 1969

Beneath the blazing sun's relentless heat
*   men and flocks are sweltering,*
*   pines are scorched.*
We hear the cuckoo's voice; then sweet songs of the turtle dove and
*   finch are heard.*
Soft breezes stir the air....but threatening north wind sweeps them
*   suddenly aside. The shepherd trembles, fearful of violent storm*
*   and what may lie ahead.*
    —Antonio Vivaldi, *L'Estate, Allegro non molto*

"Good morning!" he said to the girl on the bench. She was looking at the bright white clouds in the powder blue sky and drawing in her sketchbook. "Or should I say, *'Buongiorno, Signorina'?* I just arrived. From the airport. On the water bus. Hot day, isn't it?"

She glanced at him then turned her head up, again looking intently at the clouds and sketching.

"I'm sorry," he said. "Do you speak English? I'm American."

"How could I tell?" she said, still looking up. "Look at that cloud. The big one. There. What do you see? Is it a horse or a cow?"

"Ah, you *do* speak English."

30

"Well? A horse or a cow? Or maybe a dog? Or a sheep? What do you see?"

"It's a cumulus," he said.

"Smart aleck! I know it's a cumulus. You think because I'm a girl, I don't know a cumulus cloud from a cirrus. Do you know Shelley?"

"The poet?"

"The poet."

"No, not personally."

"He wrote from the point of view of the cloud:
I bring fresh showers for the thirsting flowers,
    From the seas and the streams;
I bear light shade for the leaves when laid
    In their noonday dreams.
From my wings are shaken the dews that waken
    The sweet buds every one,
When rocked to rest on their mother's breast,
    As she dances about the sun.
I wield the flail of the lashing hail,
    And whiten the green plains under,
And then again I dissolve it in rain,
    And laugh as I pass in thunder.
Would you like to hear it in Italian?"

He looked up at the clouds again. "No. I wouldn't understand a word of it. A horse, I think. A long neck," he said. "Longer than a cow. Bigger than a dog. Or a sheep."

"Yes, that's what I see," she said. "Definitely a horse. On the other hand, it could be a giraffe." She smiled.

The young man laughed. "I suppose it could be a giraffe. So, are you visiting? Traveling? Sketching your way through Europe on vacation?"

31

"I live here," she said, continuing to look skyward. "Yes. Definitely a giraffe. Do you know Bellini?"

"Should I?"

"One of Venice's greatest painters. He painted clouds. Many of them. You should go to the *Gallerie dell'Accademia*. Look for the *Pieta*. Or the *Virgin and Child* at the *Museo Correr*. You see clouds everywhere in Venice. Giovanni Bellini. His father, Jacopo Bellini. Andrea Mantegna. Vittore Carpaccio. Titian. But Titian liked nudes, too."

He laughed. "Thank you for the art history lesson. So, you live in Italy?"

"*Here*," she said. "I live *here*, in Venice."

"Wow! You're lucky," he said. "To live here, in Venice, I mean. I've heard so much about it. I'm from Brooklyn. That's in New York."

"I know." She looked at his face. Good looking, she thought. Nice smile. "That's where I was born. Brooklyn." She couldn't resist. "That's in New York!" she said. "Sorry, just teasing."

"You were born in Brooklyn! Really?"

"Really." She liked his smile, the curl of his lips. It was a generous smile, an honest smile. Not like so many other men whose smiles were contrived, not honest, not real. She could tell a lot about a man from his smile. A woman, too, for that matter.

"Wow! That's cool. What a coincidence. Here we are, thousands of miles from home and we meet in Venice."

"Thousands of miles from *your* home. Just a mile from *my* home." She looked back at the cloud. "Definitely a giraffe," she said, as she sketched the head and long neck.

"I wonder if you could help a fellow Brooklynite," he said. "I've never been here before. I left rather in a hurry. I don't even have a map. I'm looking for the Grand Canal."

"You've come to the right place," she said. She looked at his dark brown eyes. Kind eyes, she thought. Pleasant face. And handsome. All that and a nice smile. "There it is," she said, pointing her pencil to the right. "Just walk that way and if you fall into the water, you'll have found the Grand Canal."

"I'll try not to fall into the water. I'm a good swimmer, but I'd prefer to remain dry for a while. Actually, I'm looking for a house that's supposed to be right on the Grand Canal," he said.

"A particular house, or just any house? There are many houses along the Grand Canal. Small ones. Large ones. Mostly large ones."

"I don't know if it's small or large. I'm looking for the house of my uncle and aunt. I understand it's called *Palazzo Palladio.*"

She was startled. "*Palazzo Palladio?* Who are you?" she asked.

"My name is David. David Tomlinson. May I ask your name?"

"Tomlinson? *You're* David Tomlinson?"

"Yes. My uncle is Ben Tomlinson. My aunt is Serafina."

"You're David Tomlinson."

"That's right. Do you know my uncle and aunt? Benjamin and Serafina Tomlinson?"

"I *should* know them. They're my parents."

"Your parents! You must be Angelica!"

33

She dropped her pencil and sketch pad and jumped to her feet and wrapped her arms around him. "Angelica. Yes. Angelica Tomlinson. Your cousin. I've been reading your letters for years. They're always so positive. So full of hope. Now I recognize you from your photographs. Your hair is much longer than in the photographs. I didn't know you were coming."

"It was sudden," he said. "And I should have recognized you from the photographs your father has been sending of his family. You look a lot like your mother."

"No. My mother is *beautiful*. She's one-hundred percent Venetian. I'm a mutt. A little of this, a little of that."

"No," he said. "You're lovely. I almost didn't approach you. I thought maybe you were a model. Or a movie star. On vacation."

"Well, you certainly know how to flatter a girl! But I'm surprised to see you. And glad. So, you graduated from college last month? Some kind of engineering?"

"Civil," he said. "Civil engineering. I like to build things. Bridges, roads, pipelines. Ever since I was a little boy, I liked to build things. You were going to be an architect?"

"I got my degree in architecture at *Università Iuav di Venezia,* but I don't like drawing a lot of straight lines. So, I switched to art. My Papa's a civil engineer," she said. "Your Uncle Benjamin. He studied engineering in America. In Pittsburgh. Before the war. He met Mamma during the war. After the war, they got married and settled here in Venice. It's Mamma's home. Papa helped rebuild the roads and bridges in Northern Italy. The war made a mess. He set up his own engineering firm. Now he's working on a project to keep Venice from being swallowed up by the sea."

"Maybe I can help," he said. "We studied the case of Venice at MIT. It's serious. We looked at the data on rising sea levels and the effects they're having on the buildings here and other places around the world. Some coastal cities will disappear in the next fifty years. Whole island nations will vanish, like Maldives in the Indian Ocean. I have some ideas about Venice that I can share with your father. But first I'll have to find a place to stay."

"Don't be silly. You'll stay with us. As long as you want. Mamma and Papa will love to have you." 'So will I,' she thought to herself. "We have lots of room. I'm sure Papa would like to hear some new approaches," she said. "How long can you stay?"

"Indefinitely," he said. "I've heard Venice is a nice place. Nice weather, even in the winter. Much nicer than Massachusetts. Or Brooklyn. And all that delicious Italian food. I love Italian food, and…and… Actually, I'm not planning to return to America."

"Does it have something to do with Vietnam?"

"It has everything to do with Vietnam," he said. "My college deferment is expiring. My classmates are getting drafted or going to grad school or working for the military-industrial complex. I don't want to fight or go on to grad school, and I'm absolutely not going to sell my soul to the war profiteers. I'm not a coward. I'd fight in a just war. But not this war. This is a criminal war."

"I understand," she said. "It's a terrible war. So much bombing. So many dead. People here wonder why the Americans are fighting the poor people of Vietnam in their own country. Some Americans are here to avoid being drafted. Even some soldiers who left their units."

"Will they understand? Your mother and father, I mean? They were heroes in World War Two. I've read about them in magazine articles. They might not understand."

"They'll understand. Mamma was a partisan. She fought Mussolini's Fascists and then Hitler's Nazis when she was younger than I am now. She opposes the Vietnam War. Papa does, too. He says it's a stupid war. There are no Italian units there. Italians know something about war."

"I'm glad to hear that," he said. "My father has disowned me. He supports the war. He got a commission in the Air Force Reserve after law school, but he never actually served on active duty. I tried to argue with him, but he wraps himself in the flag and calls me a traitor."

"And your mother?"

"She supports my father. She says I should go to Italy and live with my Communist aunt."

"My mother? They think Mamma's a Communist?"

"They do. My father was still living at home with my grandparents in Brooklyn Heights when Uncle Benjamin and your mother came after the war. He thinks your mother turned Uncle Ben into a Communist."

She shook her head. "Let's walk through the Piazza San Marco to my house," she said. "It's not far. Is that all you have, just your backpack?"

"I left in a hurry," he said. "It was a last-minute decision. To leave home, I mean."

They started walking from the front of the Danieli Hotel past the Doge's Palace. "It's a beautiful building, don't you think?" she asked.

"Spectacular," he said. "I've seen pictures, but it's more impressive in real life. Much bigger than I thought."

"And probably more tourists than you thought!" The lines of visitors waiting to enter the building went on for hundreds of meters. Europeans, Americans, Asians.

"How far is your house?" he asked.

"Not far. Maybe ten minutes. It's a nice place. You'll like the architecture."

"And it's on the Grand Canal?"

"It is. And we have a nice view of the *Ponte di Rialto*, the Rialto Bridge. You must have seen pictures of it, even in America."

"It's famous," he said. "We studied all sorts of bridges. The Rialto is one of the oldest. Solid. Well designed. And I understand there are even shops on the bridge."

"There have always been businesses on the bridge," she said. "Remember Shylock in *The Merchant of Venice*? Our family has owned a shop on the Rialto Bridge for many years, even during the Fascist and the Nazi occupation. My *Nonna*, my grandmother, had a shop she used to support the partisans."

"Shylock," he said. "The Jewish money lender. I remember from high school English literature class. Shakespeare called it a comedy, but it wasn't much of a comedy from the Jewish perspective. The play was very anti-Semitic. Is there much anti-Semitism in Venice these days?"

"Oh, there's always some, but not like it used to be," she said. "There are five synagogues in the city. Over there, in the Ghetto. Most Jewish people live outside the Ghetto."

"I experienced some prejudice in school. Just some bigots. I never wanted to get involved in anything religious. How about you? Do you go to a synagogue? Or a church?" he asked.

"Neither. We're not religious. Nonna's my grandmother. She's a lapsed Catholic. She wants to know where God was when Mussolini and Hitler were murdering millions of people. Mamma and Papa are total atheists. I guess I'm an agnostic. I could be convinced, I suppose, if someone would ever show me some hard evidence of a supernatural being or an extra-terrestrial, but I haven't seen any evidence of any of that stuff. Virgin birth, turning water into wine, and all that. It's mythology. Organized religion has done incredible harm to people all over the world. It's big business, all for profit. I like the art and the music, but the superstition, no. I don't buy it. You?"

"My parents are mixed, like yours. Dad was raised Jewish. Mom was raised Lutheran. They argue a lot."

"My parents don't argue. Papa says they have a democratic marriage. Each has one vote, and Mamma has the tiebreaker! They laugh a lot."

"I think I'll like them. I'm already glad I came."

She took his hand and quickened their pace across the *Piazza. "Benvenuti a Venezia, Cugino David!"*

Death Comes to Burano

The Lace Mill

Mid-Summer

His limbs are now awakened from their repose
by fear of lightning's flash and thunder's roar,
as gnats and flies buzz furiously around.
  —Antonio Vivaldi, *L'Estate, Adagio e piano - Presto e forte*

"I know you," Chiara Donati said.

"Really?"

The neatly dressed man walked slowly out of the shadows from the back of the mill toward Chiara's chair. He stopped in front of her and looked down, as she worked her needle in and out of the piece. She looked up from her work for a glance at the man's sharp-featured face, then returned to the lace piece on her lap.

"I've seen you here in the mill. Every time you come, a lace maker dies."

"Well, then, you know why I'm here."

"I know," she said. "Everybody knows."

"Everybody?"

"Everybody. Last year, you came for my best friend, Donatella Tetrucci."

"Yes, I remember Donatella," he said. "She was very old."

"We were born in the same year."

"Ah, yes," he said, nodding.

39

"All our lives we lived here on this island. We grew up together. Our mothers were best friends. We were in school together. We took First Communion together. In the Church of San Martino. You know, here on Burano."

"It's good to have friends," he said.

"One morning, she saw you walking down the street, next to the canal, and she tried to get away."

"There is no getting away," he said. He had a soft voice, not at all unpleasant.

"No getting away," she said. "You know your job."

"I've been doing this job for a long time," he said.

"I've been doing *my* job for a long time, too. Right here. In this mill. In this very corner of the room. More than ninety years I have been here doing my job," she said.

"A fleeting moment," he said.

"Sometimes it seems that way to me," Chiara said. "Just a fleeting moment."

"Like a flash of lightning," he said.

The mill has been on *Fondamenta Cao di Rio a Destra* on the *Riva dei Santi* for more years than anyone can remember. Outside the mill, the sky darkened and a heavy rain came down on the streets and canals of Burano. A flash of lightning lit up the man's face, chalky white.

"They call you *Inevitabile*," she said. "Everyone here. That's what they call you."

"Do they now?"

"*Si. Signor Inevitabile*. That's what the people call you. *Inevitabile*. Like the seasons. You come and you go. Like the seasons. Summer comes, and summer goes. Autumn comes and goes. And winter. Then spring, and it starts all over again. *Inevitabile*."

"I like that," he said. "*Signor Inevitabile*. I like that. I'm known by many names, but this one feels right. I like it. Thank you."

"I suppose people do try to get away. When they see you coming."

He smiled. It was not a cruel smile. It was a smile of understanding. Chiara was not afraid.

"You wouldn't believe the tricks they try," he said.

"What kind of tricks?" she asked.

"All kinds. Some take potions. Some run. They cry. Most of them pray."

"They pray?"

"Fervently," he replied.

"And it makes no difference?"

"What do you think?" he asked.

"I thought it might make a difference," she said. "If they prayed."

"It makes no difference," he said.

"Maybe it makes them more comfortable," she said. Chiara had given up praying more than seventy years ago, when her baby died.

"You may be right," he said. "But that's all it does. Gives them a little comfort. I don't mind. You must believe, I'm not cruel. I just have a job to do. We all have our jobs. Don't you see? Some jobs require many years of training. Some not so much. My job requires a certain degree of diplomacy, of sensitivity."

"You wouldn't take them in the middle of their prayer? Maybe you wait until they finish their prayer? Sometimes? If they are sincere?"

"No. As I said, it makes no difference."

"Because they're not praying to you? Maybe if they were praying to you it might make a difference?"

"No. It would make no difference. I don't pay any attention. When it's time, it's time."

"*Signor Inevitabile*," she said.

"*Sono io*. That's me," he said.

"*Signor Inevitabile*. That's you."

Chiara looked into his eyes. They were kind eyes. She could respect someone with kind eyes. Too often, she had known men with anger and hate in their hearts, or greed or lust, or pride, and she could see it in their eyes. Not this one. This one had kind eyes.

"You don't mind my asking so many questions?"

"I don't mind at all. I enjoy conversations like this with intelligent humans. It's rare to find someone who is both intelligent and curious. Many people think they're intelligent, but they're not curious. Those people are not so interesting."

"You paid me a compliment," she said. "You called me intelligent."

"I don't mind saying so. If it's true. And it's true," he said. "I know you, Chiara Donati. I knew your mother and your father. They were also intelligent."

"And my baby? Did you know my baby girl?"

"Yes, I knew her. Briefly." he said. "I didn't want to take your baby, my dear Chiara. I never want to take a baby. But there was something wrong. Your baby was too small. She came too soon."

"I was too young. I was a baby myself."

"I know it's no comfort to you, Chiara, but you should know I took the man who violated you."

"He was an evil man," she said. "*Il male. Molto brutto.*"

"Very bad, indeed. That was the last time he hurt anyone. I can assure you, Chiara. I had no hesitation in taking him. I took him that very night. Your world is better off without him."

Chiara could never forget that steamy August night as she walked from the mill to her home on *Calle Baracche*. She pleaded with him not to hurt her, but she saw hate in his eyes. She was twelve years old. She had never known there could be such evil in the world. That there could be such evil in Burano.

Chiara stopped crying many years ago.

"Well, then, tell me, *Signor Inevitabile,* if you don't mind my asking, is it true sometimes you must wait?"

"Wait? Yes, sometimes I wait for the right time."

"The right time?"

"Time for me is different from time for you."

"Time is time," she said. "A second, a minute, an hour, a day, a month, a year. Ten years. A hundred years. It's all the same for me. How can time be different for you?"

"Oh, it's very different. I'll give you an example. How long would you say we've been talking here this morning, just now?"

"Five minutes, maybe ten," she said.

"For you, five or ten minutes," he said. "For me, the blink of an eye."

"The blink of an eye?"

"An instant. Less than an instant. You might say, in no time at all."

"I'm afraid I don't understand," she said, not looking up from her work.

"You don't understand?" he asked. "What is it you don't understand? Is my Italian so bad? You know, I speak many languages."

"Your Italian is fine. But you're speaking in riddles. If you want people to understand, you must speak plainly."

He laughed. "There are not many who could admonish me as well as you, my dear. Of course, you are right. I should speak more plainly."

"Well," she said, "in any event, I understand you have a rule."

"I have many rules," he said.

"You have many rules?"

"I have many rules. Rules for *who*. Rules for *when*. Not so much *how*, though. That's not in my department. That requires a certain amount of technical knowledge."

"Is it true, then? You have a rule you will not take a lace maker until she's finished the piece she's working on?"

"Well," he said, "it's not actually a rule. More like a preference. I have always respected the lace makers. Such beauty. Such delicate work. I don't like to interfere when someone is creating such exquisitely beautiful things as Venetian lace. I'm not a cruel man."

She laughed. "You're not a man at all."

"Sometimes I look like a man."

"And other times?"

"Sometimes a woman. Sometimes a child. Or an animal."

"Like a snake, I hear. But we have no snakes on Burano. You couldn't come as a snake."

"Sometimes I come as a gull," he said. "Burano has many gulls. Sometimes they just sit on the *Canale di Burano*."

"There are too many gulls on the *Canale di Burano*," she said. "Sometimes I think they're a nuisance, but they were here before we came. So, it's all right."

"Sometimes I join the gulls on the smaller canals. Waiting. You may have seen me, sitting on the water, waiting, along with the other gulls. I like the company of gulls. They are chatty. We have lively conversations. They do enjoy their gossip. You wouldn't believe the stories they tell, especially about the lovers under the bridges and on the beaches. Oh, my! There are so many gulls here."

"And visitors," she added. "We have many visitors. They come in to see how we make the lace. They take pictures and ask questions. You could be mistaken for a visitor."

"I could, but I'm not a visitor. I'm much better dressed, don't you think? No, not visiting. I'm working," he said. "Like you. Working. You've been working here at the mill for many years. I know. I see you every time I come to the mill."

"I came to the mill when I was eight years old," she said. "I grew up here. This has been home for me, all my life. I have never left the island. I have no need for the rest of the world. This is my work. Making lace. That's what I do. What I have done since I was a child."

"Child labor," he said. "Tsk, tsk. Those capitalists!"

"My mother said I would get a good education, a practical education."

"Making lace," he said.

"*Sì*. Making lace. About how to make beautiful lace, *merletto bello*. And about life. Mamma said the ladies in the mill would teach me everything I need to know about life."

"And did they? Did they teach you about life? The ladies?"

"About life in the mill," she said. "And in Burano. How to get along. How to live. Here on this island."

"And the rest of Venice? The rest of Italy? The world? What have the ladies taught you about the rest of the world, Chiara?"

"This is my world," she said. "It's enough. I have everything I need, right here. It's enough for me."

"You may not believe it, but I worry about you."

"You worry about me? Why?"

"Well, you know, many of the women at the mental asylum at San Clemente are listed as lace makers. Maybe it happens because of the demanding work they do. The work you do. So careful. No mistakes. Maybe it drives the women insane."

"Don't put me in that category," she said. "I'm not a lunatic. I love the work I do. I create beauty with every stitch. Look at my work. Is it not beautiful? So delicate. So intricate."

"Yes, your work is exquisite. There's no denying it. Even so, you must be tired," he said. "After all these years, aren't you tired, Chiara? You work so hard. Every day. Every time I come to this mill, I look over at you, and you're always busy making lace. Don't you get tired?"

"Sometimes I get tired," she said.

"I can give you rest," he said.

"Hah! I know your kind of rest. No, thank you. I don't need your kind of rest."

"Are you sure, Chiara? Are you so sure?"

"I'm sure. I have much more to do."

"I'll wait. I'll wait until you finish this piece."

"It's a big piece. It's for the grand table in the Doge's Palace in the *Piazza San Marco*. It could take weeks. Maybe months. It must be perfect. Who knows? It could take years for such a magnificent piece."

"Weeks," he said. "Months. Years. It's all the same to me. Finish your lace, Signora Chiara. I'll be back another time. Maybe I'll stop by to have another conversation with you. When I'm in the neighborhood."

"Conversation?"

"That's all. Until your lace is completed."

Chiara continued to work on her table cloth for the grand table of the Doge's Palace, perhaps a little more slowly, a little more deliberately, to be flawless, perhaps taking just a bit more care with each stitch.

Pelletteria Tedeschi

The Rialto Bridge

Friday, September 17, 1943

Alas, his worst fears were justified, as the heavens roar and great hailstones beat down upon the proudly standing corn.
—Antonio Vivaldi, *L'Estate, Presto*

"What are you doing, Paolo?" Rose Palladio asked. "Why did you use the back door?"

The thin young man darted behind a rack of long leather coats.

"Hide me, Rose! They're coming after me."

"Who's coming after you?"

"The German pigs. They're looking for me. You have to hide me. Down below. In the special hiding place. Hurry, Rose! Before they come."

The place where the Pelletteria Tedeschi, the German leather goods shop, now stood had seen many businesses over the past three centuries – money lending, fruits and vegetables, fabrics – but one thing had remained. When Antonio da Ponte designed and built the bridge, he included, with his own hands and without the knowledge of the workers, a secret chamber under the place where now the Pelleteria Tedeschi shop stood, a chamber that would hide refugees from persecution by the government, the church, and, now, the Nazis. Only a few Venetians, and none of the outsiders, knew the secret.

"I stabbed a Nazi major under the *Ponte San Tonio*. I think I killed him, Rose. I'm sure I killed the pig. He was going to arrest me and send me to the camps. I had no choice."

"A major? Major Geyer? You killed Major Geyer? The SS officer in charge?"

"*Si!* That one," he whispered. "The one they call 'The Vulture, *L'avvoltoio.'* He was a bad man, Rose, *un uomo cattivo.* You know what he did, this Nazi monster? He demanded Professor Jona hand over a list of Jews in the district. He was going to round them up and send them to the camps."

"Professor Jona gave up on religion a long time ago," Rose said. "But he agreed to serve the community."

Professor Giuseppe Jona was a distinguished physician and professor of medicine. He was also the President of the Jewish Community in Venice since 1940. The Nazis now occupying Mestre and Venice declared Jews to be foreigners of a hostile nationality and determined to murder them all in pursuit of Adolf Hitler's "final solution," the systematic eradication of Jews, Slavs, and all others not considered to be worthy of living.

"The Professor said he needed time to collect all the names. Then he went to his home and burned all the papers with names of Jews, then he injected himself with a lethal dose of morphine. Professor Jona committed suicide rather than give Geyer a list of the Jews in Venice. Nearly eighty years old. He couldn't survive the camps, and he couldn't betray the people. He's a hero, Rose. A great hero. He will never be forgotten. He sacrificed his own life so many others would be spared."

Rose crossed herself, a reflex action, as she no longer believed in what she called the superstitious nonsense of the church. Where was God when the Nazis came? Where were the priests? Where was the Pope? Rose could not continue to believe in a god who is omniscient, who knows what is going on, and does nothing to stop it.

"A hero," she said. Rose knew Professor Jona well. She was the beneficiary of his professional treatment at the hospital when she had a difficult delivery. He saved her life and the life of her baby daughter. She has returned the favor over the years by anonymously donating money to support his work at the hospital.

"Hurry, Rose. Hide me."

"Follow me," she said quietly, as she moved to a far corner of the shop with no window, behind racks of black leather coats. "And be quiet."

Hidden from view of passersby on the steps of the bridge, she pushed aside a work table and stepped hard on a board on the floor, unlocking a trap door with a slight click. She lifted the trap door and motioned for Paolo to climb down the ladder.

"There's enough food and water for many weeks," she whispered to the fugitive. "Maybe until the Germans are gone. But be quiet. Absolutely quiet. Not a sound. Not a peep. Not a cough or a sneeze. Understand?"

"I understand. *Grazie*, Rose! *Dio ti benedica!*" he whispered, as he climbed down the ladder.

"God bless us all, Paolo," she said, as she lowered the trap door and snapped the lock by pressing hard on the other end of the floorboard.

"Except for the Nazi pigs," she muttered to herself. "God, whoever or whatever you are, listen! No blessings for the Nazi pigs! You hear me? If you made these monsters, you should be ashamed of yourself."

She returned to the front of the shop and busied herself rearranging the clothing on the racks. The occupiers allowed the shop to remain open because it traded with German businesses in the homeland – and it had a German name.

In what would surely go down in history as one of the great deceptions of the war, Rose Palladio had never given any indication of resistance to the occupation. Strictly business, she always said. But her real business these days was supporting the partisans who sabotaged the German communications and supply lines. She used no radio, only person-to-person communication. And most of the "persons" were members of her family or life-long friends. She was godmother to some of the operatives, including young Paolo Padovano. All were members of centuries-old Venetian families, like her own, families whose ties to Venice go back hundreds of years.

"*Guten Abend werte Dame.*"

"*Buona sera, il capitano.*" Rose managed a smile as the young German officer entered the shop.

"You have a most lovely shop, *Signora*. Many beautiful German things."

"*Si, il capitano.* Maybe you would like to buy something for yourself or for your wife."

"I have no wife, *Signora*."

"Or maybe lady friend? A pretty *fraulein*?"

"No, no. No wife, no girlfriend. My loyalty is just to *mein Fuehrer*, Adolph Hitler."

"So, I give you a nice coat. Soon it will be cold. You will need a nice coat. Here, up front, there are some beautiful leather coats just your size."

"I couldn't accept such a thing. It would be a bribe," he said.

"What bribe? You wear it as a uniform. I make it just like a regulation coat. No one will tell the difference. Is anyone with you here? Now?"

"No. I'm alone. Everyone is looking for a murderer," he said.

"A murderer!" she whispered. "Who is murdered, *il capitano*? An Italian thief, maybe?"

"I wish it were," he said. "No, it is our Major, Major Geyer."

"No, you don't say. Major Geyer, our Commandant. He was just in here yesterday. I gave him a nice coat."

"We must find the killer. We *will* find him. He can't get away."

"Where did it happen, this killing?" she asked.

"East of here. Under the San Tonio bridge," he said. "We think the murderer ran toward *Piazza San Marco*, where he could get a boat. That's where all my soldiers are going. We'll catch him. Then we'll hang him in the Piazza. It will be a public hanging. Of course, first we will get all the information we want from him – it will be bad for him."

"Of course, *il capitano*. He must be dealt with strictly," she said. "I didn't hear any shots."

"The killer used a knife. He cut the major's throat," he said.

"*Dio mio!*" she said, crossing herself. "*Terribile!* What does this killer look like?"

"Nobody saw him. I assume it was a man, but it could have been a woman."

"Ah," she said, "it could have been a woman? Maybe a prostitute? So many prostitutes walking around the city these days. Shameful! These young women. They should be ashamed of themselves. Walking around in the dark. Do you think it could have been a prostitute, *il capitano*? There have been many prostitutes lately."

"Maybe," he said. "Well, *Signora*, if you hear anything, you will let us know."

"*Certo, il capitano*," she said. "Most certainly."

"Well, good night, *Signora*. Keep your eyes and ears open."

"*Si, il capitano*," she said. "*Buona notte.* Good night."

As he headed to the door, the captain turned. "What was that?" he asked.

"*Signore?*" she said. She had heard it, too. It was the sound of someone snoring.

"Is someone here? In the back?" he asked. "I hear a noise. From the back of the shop."

"Oh, no, *il capitano*," she said. "I can assure you we are alone. Maybe a dog or a cat outside on the bridge. That must be it. They come around looking for some scraps of food. Sometimes they make noises."

"There is someone back there," he said. He opened the clasp of his holster and drew out his Luger as he walked to the back of the shop. "Come out!" he shouted.

He pushed his way past the racks of leather coats and noticed a slight crack in the floor under the work table.

53

"*Was ist das?*" he asked, as he pushed the table aside. He stomped on the floorboards around the crack until he heard the snap. He reached down and started to open the trap door.

Rose grabbed a pair of large shears from the work table and plunged it deep into the back of the captain's neck. He slumped over and fell heavily to the floor. She lifted the trap door and pushed the body into the opening. It fell the four meters and landed with a thud on the floor of the secret hiding place.

Paolo woke and tumbled from his cot.

Rose turned off the lights in the shop, placed a "Closed" sign on the door and locked it. She climbed down the ladder, sliding the trap door above her.

"Paolo," she whispered from the ladder. "Make sure he's dead."

With only the light from one small tealight candle, he made his way to the body of the German officer and felt his neck for a pulse.

"He's dead, Rose. You killed him."

"I had no choice," she said. "Now we must get rid of the body. Back here, through this tunnel, there is an old well. Drag him this way." Rose led the way, hunched over. Paolo followed, dragging the captain's body. When they got to the well, Rose said, "Help me to slide this stone cover." Together, they pushed the heavy cover aside.

"Throw him in," Rose said. Paolo lifted the body and dropped it into the old well. It dropped some ten meters before they could hear the thump of the body hitting the bottom of the dry well. She threw in the bloody shears.

"Now we slide the cover back," she said. They pushed the stone cover back over the well.

"Rose," Paolo said, "you killed a German officer. Two German officers in one night!"

"They're not the first," she said. "With the help of the Allies and the partisans, there will be many more."

"The Germans will be looking for him," Paolo said.

"In the morning, they'll be searching for him," Rose said. "I'll arrange for the shop to be filled with our friends. You will come up and mingle with them. Everyone will have an alibi. You tell them you were with me all day working in the shop, right?"

"Right," he replied. "I was here all day working with the *Signora*."

"Cleaning and arranging the coats," she said.

"Cleaning and arranging the coats," he repeated.

"And leave your brown coat down here. Put on a black leather jacket. If anyone managed to see you running, they will say a man with a brown coat. What about the knife?" she asked.

"I threw it in the canal."

"Good. Now I'll go up and see if there is any blood on the floor. Meanwhile, stay awake. You can sleep tomorrow. And move the cot way over there, just in case you fall asleep and start snoring again."

She climbed the ladder and looked for any signs of blood. It was a clean stab. No traces of blood on the floor. Just to be sure she hadn't missed any spots, she covered the door with a heavy rug that had been rolled up and stored in a corner. She lifted the work table back in its place.

The next day went as planned. Rose had called a dozen of her family and friends and arranged for them to be at the shop by morning opening time, ten o'clock. She posted a neatly lettered sign advertising a special sale: Everything 50%! *Promozione di vendita speciale. Tutto al 50%!* The shop was packed when the German corporal entered. He was deferential and was trying hard to improve his Italian language skills.

"*Buongiorno, la signora Palladio,*" he said, with a polite bow in Rose's direction. "*Come stai?* Did I say it correctly, *Signora?* I want to know Italian very well. After the war, I want to be a teacher. A foreign language teacher. Italian and French especially. Such beautiful languages."

"*Buongiorno,*" she said. "*Guten Morgen mein Freund. Wie geht es dir?* Welcome to the *Pelletteria Tedeschi,* the best German leather shop in all Italy. Have you come to take advantage of our special sale? Everything fifty percent. You won't find better prices anywhere. High quality merchandise made in Germany."

Rose had met the young man in the Rialto market. He had introduced himself as Christofer. "My father is Italian, Signora, so I am named for the great Italian explorer, Cristoforo Colombo." Now it was official business the corporal had in mind.

"No, *Signora*, thank you anyway," he said. "I have come on some important business matter."

"Oh, I thought maybe you came to buy a nice German leather coat. Corporal," she whispered. "I can make you a special deal. Seventy-five percent. What do you think? Is that an attractive offer?"

"Seventy-five percent?"

"To tell you the truth," she said, "I would be losing money, but such a nice young man. We want to show our hospitality. How about it? You won't find a better deal anywhere."

"May I ask your guests a few questions?"

"Of course," she said. "Has something happened in the city?"

"Just some mischief," he said. "We must ask where everyone was last night."

While the young corporal went about the shop asking questions, Rose and Paolo were busy waiting on customers in a manner that must have been well rehearsed. The killing of Major Geyer would go unsolved for all time. No Venetian ever spoke of it again. Nor of the captain who went missing in Venice in September of 1943.

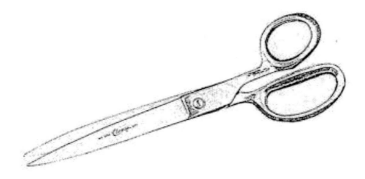

PART III. Autumn

Love on the Lido

Alberoni Beach, Lido di Venezia

Sunday, October 31, 1976

Celebrates the peasant, with songs and dances,
The pleasure of a bountiful harvest.
And fired up by Bacchus' liquor,
many end their revelry in sleep.
> —Antonio Vivaldi, *L'Autunno, Allegro*

"Happy Hallowe'en, Papa!" Angelica shouted, running across the sand. She was wearing a white Burano lace cover-up with small wings fluttering at the back. Above her head was a halo sparkling with Murano glass beads. With the sun at her back, it seemed there was an aura around her like that of Carpaccio's St. Ursula in the *Gallerie dell' Accademia*. She bent down and kissed her dozing father on the cheek and wrapped her arms around his neck. "Papa, you didn't shave today. Are you growing a beard?"

There was a bond between father and daughter composed of strands of love, respect, and admiration in both directions. Angelica loved her father for his constant nurturing, respected his life of service, and admired his integrity. Ben loved his daughter in equal measure for her devotion to her parents, respected the decisions she had made in her career as an architect and artist, and admired her integrity as she matured into a life of material success.

"That's my costume for Hallowe'en," Benjamin Tomlinson said. "I thought I would dress up as a hobo. Can't you tell?"

"Benjy," Serafina Palladio Tomlinson said, "That's not funny. You know there are so many homeless people in the world. Even women and children. How many in Italy have no home? Even in Venice, even in our *La Serenissima*. How many times have we taken in people we found lying on the steps of the Rialto Bridge? Or shivering in the *Campo San Bartolomeo* right around the corner from the church? We're lucky. We have a nice home, but many people are not so lucky. It's not something to joke about. It's a disgrace to allow such people to be without a roof over their head."

"I'm sorry, Darling. Of course, you're right. We shouldn't make fun of them."

"Well then, we should do something about it," Serafina said. "It's a problem, Benjy. You are always looking for problems to solve. So, here's a problem."

"Actually," Ben said, "I've been thinking of starting a project to build low-cost housing, maybe in Mestre, where there is vacant land. Or even scattered around the islands. There's enough room for many of these houses." Ben had been thinking in recent months of a project he and his engineering classmates had worked on in college before the war. Millions of young military veterans would be coming home after the war and would be looking for affordable housing to start their families. Such housing could be built, Ben and his group found, using simple architectural designs and low-cost locally available materials. Bill Levitt built on a large scale after the war, in New York, Pennsylvania, and Maryland. He even built a development in Puerto Rico.

"That would be a good way to spend your time," Fina said. "Instead of reading the magazines and listening to music all day. You should stay busy. Do that project. You could help thousands of people. Millions. All over the world. Remember, Angelica is an architect. She can help. You'll be a team. A new generation of Family Palladio. Wouldn't that be grand?"

Serafina Palladio Tomlinson had taken art classes at Pratt Institute in Brooklyn while she was recovering from extensive reconstructive surgery on the leg that was severely damaged during the war. She concentrated on portraits and had become Venice's premier portrait artist. Her commissions and family name assured her success.

"Actually," Angelica said, "I've been reading about some new methods of construction using recycled plastics, cardboard, and other materials. They're stronger than bricks and concrete blocks. We could build a small factory to make the materials, all from local sources. We could make the materials here and use them to build low-cost housing. We could start with small units, maybe one bedroom, and add modules to accommodate larger families. Papa and David and I can do the planning and the building, and Mamma can help with the financing from wealthy families.

"Ah, you see?" Fina said. "Already a partnership. We get such good ideas when we get out of the house into the fresh air!"

The salty smell of the sea and the bright sun with a few white clouds against a pale blue sky made this annual weekend excursion a joy for the Palladio-Tomlinson family. A picnic lunch, a few beach towels, and a folding chair was all they needed.

Ben's Riva powerboat took them from *Palazzo Palladio* down the Grand Canal past the *Gallerie dell'Accademia* and the Peggy Guggenheim, around the tip of *La Giudecca*, and across the lagoon to *Santa Maria Elisabetta* on the west side of the long, narrow Lido. Rather than take the boat around the northern – or longer southern – tip of the island, they would take a bus for the five-minute ride to the beaches on the east side. Their favorite was the *Alberoni Beach*, especially in the autumn, when most of the tourists had abandoned the Lido beaches for Ruskin's *Stones of Venice* and the bright lights and night life of the city.

Ben sat cross-legged on a bright yellow beach towel on the sand. He looked up and smiled at his daughter.

"Happy Hallowe'en, my beautiful Angel!" he said. "The brightest angel on the Lido. Come, sit a while."

The Lido is a long sandbar in the Lagoon, the only place in Venice with automobile and bus traffic. Its beaches on the Adriatic Sea are popular with tourists from all over the world who stay in the local hotels during the summer months. Those who live in Venice prefer the seaside on those clear autumn days when the skies are powder blue, the clouds are soft and white, and the summer heat has ended.

"Who needs imaginary angels when we have our own real Angel?" Fina said. "We don't need an imaginary Heaven. Here is our Heaven. A loving family on a beautiful beach with the sun shining on blue waters."

Fina was sitting in a brown canvas chair, her legs covered with a large beach towel. She looked up at her daughter and smiled the smile of a mother who marveled at the miracle of the life she had brought into the world.

When Fina, as an eighteen-year-old partisan warrior, thought she would die in the forest, she could not have imagined such a miracle. She would never stop being grateful for her life – and the life of her daughter. "And a beautiful Angel who paints clouds," she said.

Angelica reached over and took her mother's hand. "I like architecture, and – with all due modesty – I'm good at it, if I must say so myself. I like building things. But I really enjoy painting clouds. They're like the faces of people, never the same. Look. See that cloud," she said, pointing up and over the sea at a clearly defined cumulus. "Look. Up there. Doesn't that cloud look like Papa?"

"Your mother paints portraits – for which, by the way, people are willing to pay a great deal of money. You paint whatever you want, *Tesoro*," Ben said, smiling. "Hm. You know, it *does* look a little like me!" He laughed.

"Your grandfather painted lots of clouds, Angelica," David said. "Your father, Aunt Fina. I've seen some of his paintings at *La Scuola Grande di San Rocco*. His landscapes are the best of the collection. He didn't do much religious art, as many other Venetian painters did. He seemed to prefer scenes of nature."

"He was a great painter," Serafina said. "He was admitted to *La Scuola* at the age of twelve. He had such promise. You know, he also did portraits. He had a talent for portraits. I may have inherited some of that talent."

"I read your mother's book, Aunt Fina," David said. "It's a great book. The stories are fascinating. Especially the stories about your father. He was a man of great courage. He stood up for his convictions. He made no secret of his opposition to Fascism."

"No secret at all," Fina said. "He went to Milan to join the protest in 1942 and got arrested. He died in prison."

"Murdered by Mussolini's thugs," Angelica said. "It must have been a terrible time for you, Mamma."

"It was. That's when my mother and I joined the Resistance," Fina said. "So stupid they were, Mussolini and his idolaters. Every time they killed one of us, two more rose up to take his place."

"My parents had it all wrong," David said. "They thought if you oppose Fascism, you must be a Communist."

"And then there's my brother the armchair patriot," Ben said, sipping a glass of Prosecco.

"Enough!" Angelica said. "Let's go in the water. It's getting too hot here."

Angelica and David started to run to the water. Angelica threw off her cover-up, revealing a slender body with a skimpy bikini swimsuit.

"Uncle Ben? Aunt Fina?" David called. "Won't you join us?"

"You go," Ben said. "It's likely to be a little chilly for us. You youngsters go. We'll watch."

Angelica and David ran to the edge of the beach and splashed into the cool waters of the *Golfo di Venezia*.

"You don't have to hide your leg, Fina," Ben said.

"It's ugly," she said.

"It's not ugly. It's just a scar. Look. I have scars all over."

"It's different," she said.

"How is it different? Look. Here's a scar on my hip. And scars on my back."

"You're a man."

"*Grazie!* Thank you for noticing after more than thirty years."

"Has it been that long?" she asked. "Thirty years?"

"Seems like yesterday, doesn't it?"

"Like yesterday. Only better," she said.

"We survived, Fina. We came out of it. We came out of the forest. We came out of the war. Alive. Together. We came out alive, and we've made a good life, haven't we? Hasn't it been a good life, Fina? Are you happy? Have I made you happy?"

"I'm happy, Benjy. I'm very happy. All thanks to you, *mi amore.*"

"And these thirty-two years have been my reward," he said. "*Mio amore più caro,* my dearest love, *La mia Serafina della Casa del Palladio di Venezia.*"

"They have been good years, haven't they, Benjy? Since the war? Since that terrible war?"

"They've been wonderful years, *anni meravigliosi,*" he said. "And look out there. If I believed in miracles, I would definitely say, there is our miracle."

"They love each other, you know," she said.

"I know. But it's forbidden love. They're cousins. First cousins."

"Why? Why forbidden? They make a wonderful couple. She will have no other man, and he will have no other woman. Would you give your blessing?" she asked.

"It's against the law," he said. "Isn't it? For first cousins to marry?"

"No. Not in Italy."

"My brother and his wife would have apoplexy."

"Maybe this would be something they could agree on," Fina said. "Apart from thinking I'm *una Comunista*."

"Angelica Tomlinson and David Tomlinson," Ben said with a smile. "For all practical purposes, they do come from separate families. After all, she *is* a Palladio."

"She said she doesn't want children. So that wouldn't be a problem. What do you say? Will you give them your blessing?"

"If that's what they want. Sure," he said. "You're right. They do make a nice couple. Look at them."

"Here they come. Look. Holding hands," she said. "So soon!" she shouted at the couple. "How's the water?"

"Chilly," Angelica said. "You were right, Papa."

"A little on the cool side," David said. "But not too bad for the end of October."

"Here," Fina said. "Sit with us. We have something to tell you. Ben, tell them."

"Why me?" Ben asked. "It was your idea."

"You're the man of the family. You tell them."

"All right," Ben said. "Angelica, *mia cara figlia*, my dear daughter. Ben, my dear nephew. We've been talking it over. Oh, Fina, you tell them. It's your idea. Go ahead."

"Oh, all right," she said. "Angelica, your father has many fine features, but sentiment is not one of them."

"*Mamma mia*," Angelica said, "for Pete's sake what is it? What do you want to tell us?"

"Well, my dears, your father – David, your uncle – and I have decided to give you our blessing."

"Blessing? What does that mean?" Angelica asked.

"I think she means they will be happy if we want to get married," David said.

"*Sì,*" Fina said. "We will be happy if you want to marry. Even though you are cousins, it doesn't matter. We will be happy if you are happy. Yes, Ben?" Ben nodded.

David and Angelica laughed. "Aunt Fina," David said, "I'm gay."

"*Sì,*" Fina said. "We, too, are gay. We're all gay."

"No, *Mamma.* That's not what he means."

"No? *Contento, no?* Happy. Like us?" Fina said.

Ben smiled. "No, my dear, not like us."

"*Non capisco,*" she said. "I don't understand. He is gay. We are gay, too. No?"

"Mamma," Angelica said, taking Fina's hand in hers, "*Gli piacciono i ragazzi.*"

"Oh!" Fina managed. "David, you like boys?"

"Yes, Aunt Fina," David said with a smile.

"OK, then, *va bene,*" she said. "Ben, go on, go on. Give them our blessing!"

Alla vita! To life!

Campo del Ghetto Nuovo

Monday, September 24, 1945

The singing and the dancing die away
as cooling breezes fan the pleasant air,
inviting all to sleep
without a care.

—Antonio Vivaldi, *L'Autunno, Adagio molto*

"Shalom, Rabbi."

"Shalom, Tova. It's good to see you. Have a seat. How are you? Have you seen the doctor? We were all worried."

Physically, Tova had survived her ordeal. Although emaciated and anemic, she was resilient. What she had been through, what she had seen, the sights, the sounds, the smells, those would leave scars that would never heal.

"Doctor Katz says everything is all right," Tova said.

"She's a fine physician. You're in good hands," Rabbi Sam Garsten said.

Esther Katz, M.D., had graduated from the Yale School of Medicine and completed her residency in internal medicine at the Women's College Hospital in Philadelphia. She was one of few female physicians at the United States Army's 21st General Hospital, Naples. When the war ended, she visited Venice and found her calling in the Ghetto

"How about you, Rabbi?" Tova asked. "You must be tired. You do so much for the community. Especially for the elders. And the children. For all of us. You're so busy all the time. You don't get enough sleep. I feel guilty taking up your time."

"Tova, you shouldn't feel guilty about speaking with your rabbi. If I should get a little tired, I just think about you and the others and what you've been through. My service keeps me going. And I'm happy to serve this community."

"We're all happy to have our own rabbi," she said. "One time, a rabbi was brought to the camp, but he didn't stay long before they took him away."

The camp at Trieste was mainly a transit stop for those who would go on to Auschwitz. Eventually, it became a death camp, as well.

"Rabbi, is it permitted to ask a question?"

"Of course, Tova. Do you have a question?"

"Many, Rabbi," Tova replied.

In the heat of the afternoon of Thursday, August 17, 1944, the Gestapo tore the last Jewish families from their homes in *Ghetto Nuovo*. Music teacher Antonio Liuzzi and his daughter, Tova, were the last to climb the steps of the *Ponte delle Guglie* to cross the Cannaregio Canal for the walk to the *Venezia Santa Lucia* railway station.

At eleven years of age, Tova Liuzzi had been playing her violin for some five years for admiring audiences in Venice, Padua, and Verona. She had a tight grip on her violin case.

"Your mother is spared this day," Antonio said.

"We'll be all right, Papa." Tova had a glow that even the Gestapo and the SS could not dim. It was a glow that radiated from her music. Her repertoire included Bach, Beethoven, Mendelssohn, and Tchaikovsky, among others. Her favorite was Vivaldi, the Venetian master of the Baroque. She played *The Four Seasons* perfectly from memory, and she played it often. Her audiences demanded it, and she was always pleased to comply.

When they liberated the concentration camp at *La Risiera di San Sabba* in Trieste in April of 1945, soldiers of the 2nd New Zealand Division found Tova standing alone in the inner courtyard playing the opening movement of *The Four Seasons*, the Allegro in E Major. The soldiers stood and listened. And wept.

"That was lovely," the young lieutenant said.

"It's Vivaldi," Tova replied.

"You can go home. Where is your home?"

"Venice," she replied. "My home is in Venice."

"That's not far," he said. "Would you like me to take you there? We can go in my jeep. My name is Rangi," the young officer said. "Rangi Parata. Rangi means *sky* in my language, and Parata means *brother*."

"What is that language," Tova asked.

"Māori," Rangi replied. "It's the language of my people, the first people of New Zealand."

"New Zealand," Tova said. "That's far away."

"More than ten thousand miles," he said.

"You came all that way to help us."

"Yes. A long way."

"Why?" she asked.

"Why did I come all this way?"

"Yes. Why did you leave your home so far away?"

"That's a good question," he said.

"I know."

He smiled a broad smile. "You're a clever girl."

"I know," she repeated.

He laughed and held out his hand. "You know my name, Rangi. What's your name?"

"I'm called Tova," she said, shaking his hand.

"That's a beautiful name. What does it mean?"

"It's a Hebrew name. In Italian, it's like *Bella*."

"Ah!" he said. "In Māori, you would be called *Pai*."

"*Pai?*"

"It's the same as *Bella*. Maybe I will call you *Pai*."

She smiled. For the first time in a long while.

They drove the hundred miles to the Venice *Santa Lucia* Train Station, parked the jeep, and engaged a small powerboat for the half mile ride along the Grand Canal, turning left at the Cannaregio Canal to the *Ponte delle Guglie* and just a few steps to the *Campo delle Scuole*.

Tova opened her violin case, lifted the instrument, and started to play the Allegro in F Major. One by one, people opened their windows to hear Vivaldi once again in the clear air.

Tova's return to the *Ghetto Nuovo* was a mix of joy and anguish. More than two hundred had been taken in 1944, but Tova was among only eight who returned. For Tova and the others, homecoming was bittersweet. *Why me?* they asked. *Why did God spare me and not the others?* They all came to the same conclusion: *God spared me so I would tell my story to the world. So, the world would say, "Never again!"*

"Rabbi, people are saying you came from America. They say you're not a rabbi, that you're a soldier. Is it true? Did you come from America? Are you a rabbi or a soldier?"

"Yes, it's true I came from America. New York City. I *am* a rabbi, Tova, *and* a soldier. I was a chaplain in the Reserves in the United States Army. When America came into the war, I was assigned to the 88th Infantry Division. Our division came all the way from Naples."

"Did you kill Germans? Some in the community say you killed. Did you kill, Rabbi?"

"I was in an infantry division, Tova. The Germans were trying to kill us. I had to stop being a chaplain and start being a combat soldier. There came a time when I had to kill or be killed. To see some of my men being killed or kill. Yes, I killed some of them."

"Moses tells us we must not kill."

"Actually, Tova, Moses tells us not to *murder.*"

"What's the difference? Dead is dead. I saw so many dead this past year. At the camp. I don't want any more killing. God doesn't want us to kill one another. God tells us we should love life. *L'chaim*, Rabbi. *L'chaim*. Isn't that what we say? That we should treasure life and not kill?"

"Tova, we say, *L'chaim tovim ul'shalom*, for good life, for peace. It's our wish that we should all live good lives."

"I understand that, Rabbi, but the killing?"

"According to our law, the law from the Torah and the Talmud, it is permitted to defend yourself and your family and your friends. And in a just war."

"A just war?" She asked. "How do you know if a war is a just war? This war with Germany. Was it a just war?"

71

"Well, Tova, you like to ask questions. And that's good. You should always ask questions. Now let me ask you three questions. And you must think carefully before you answer."

"All right," she said. "I'm ready."

"First, you must ask yourself, is the war a last resort? Second, when we went to war against Hitler and Mussolini, was it for the right reason? And third, did we use only the means necessary to defeat the evil? If you answer yes to those questions, you have the beginning of understanding of a just war."

Tova thought about the three questions. "So, if someone is trying to kill you, or your family, or your neighbors, God says it's all right to kill him. Right?"

"It's regrettable. All killing is regrettable, but yes, you have the right to defend yourself and your family and your friends against evil. And your neighbors, even if those neighbors live in places far from your own home. That's why we Americans have traveled thousands of miles, all the way to Italy, to fight the Nazi and the Fascist. That's why I came to Italy. It was the forces of good against the forces of evil. We could not stand by and watch the horrors committed by those evil forces."

Tova looked up at the white clouds drifting above the *Ghetto Nuovo*. "And how about prisoners?" she asked. "Maybe they did something horrible in the past, but now they're not trying to kill anybody. They're in prison. How does that fit with the commandment?"

"Yes, that's a problem," the rabbi said. "Maybe it's intended to be a deterrent. If someone knows he may be executed, maybe he won't commit the crime."

"Really, Rabbi? Does anyone really believe that? Does anyone believe that some law is going to keep a man from killing another man in the heat of an argument?"

"I don't think anyone seriously believes that. It's a rationalization. When we decide we want to do something, we must have a reason, or we have to invent a reason."

"So, what *is* the reason? Tell me, Rabbi. What right does the state have to kill a man who is no longer a danger to anyone else, or to kill anyone for that matter?"

"Retaliation. An eye for an eye and a tooth for a tooth," he said. "Revenge. Like when the Nazis killed ten innocent civilians when the partisans killed one of them, or burned an entire village after an act of sabotage."

"That doesn't seem right," she said.

"I agree," the young rabbi said. "I've seen more than enough killing during the past three years."

"If a man is evil," she asked, "like Adolph Hitler, is it morally right to kill him?"

"Well, there is some difference of opinion among Jewish scholars. Some oppose all killing. Others believe such a man should be stopped before he can kill others."

"What a different world this would be if Hitler had been killed!"

"It's called *tyrannicide*, the justified killing of a tyrant."

"We heard that some of the German officers tried to kill Hitler," she said. "Last year, Rabbi. Just before the soldiers came to take us away. I heard the Commandant say some German officers tried to kill Hitler."

"They tried, several times," Rabbi Garsten said, "but they failed. In the end, he killed himself."

73

"Just one more question, Rabbi. Why do they hate us? The Christians. Why do they hate us? My father didn't do anything to them. Papa was a good man, never hurt anyone in his life. He was just a musician, a music teacher. Why did they kill him? Why do they hate us?"

Rabbi Garsten thought for a long time. He knew this was the question Jews had asked for millennia. "You ask a rational question, Tova. But it has no rational answer. Hate is not rational. It's a long story. It seems we human beings are by nature haters of anyone who is different from us. It may be easier for the wolf to live with a lamb than for the Christian and the Jew to live together."

"Isaiah," she said.

"Yes. But we survive. You survived, Tova. How did you manage?"

"The violin, Rabbi. I played waltzes mostly. They wanted happy music. The Commandant wanted Beethoven, so I played Beethoven for him. *With* him. He was a bad man but a good pianist. So, we were a duet. Violin and piano. But whatever I played, I played for Papa. Happy music or sad music, it was all for Papa."

"Happy music and Beethoven," he said with a smile. "And your father was always in your thoughts."

"Strauss and Beethoven," she said. "The guards liked *The Blue Danube*, but the Commandant liked *Für Elise*. *Moonlight Sonata*. *Violin Concerto in D major*, especially the second movement, the Largo. He would close his eyes and play. Every Friday night after his dinner. When we finished, he would give me a little treat, maybe a little bread."

"You survived," he said. "And you managed to come back to Venice."

"It's my home, Rabbi. I was born here, there, just across the *campo*, in that building, on the sixth floor. I lived there until they came for us."

"Now what, Tova?" the rabbi asked. "What will you do now?"

"I will play my music," she said. "Maybe someday, I will find the Commandant, and we can play duets again."

"You don't hate the Germans?" the rabbi asked. "After all they did? You don't hate them?"

"I don't hate anyone, Rabbi. I've seen hate. And I've seen love. Maybe in love, together, we can create something beautiful."

In April, 1976, a war crimes trial in Trieste sentenced SS-Unterscharführer Joseph Oberhauser, Commandant of La Risiera di San Sabba concentration camp, in absentia, to life imprisonment. He continued to sell beer in Munich and died November 22, 1979, at the age of 65. The Risiera is now a National Monument.

Arrivederci, Venezia!

Marco Polo Airport, Venice

Monday October 24, 2016
One Day after the Venice Marathon

The hunters emerge at dawn,
ready for the chase,
with horns and dogs and cries.
Their quarry flees while they give chase.
Terrified and wounded, the prey struggles on,
but, harried, dies.

     —Antonio Vivaldi, *L'Autunno, Allegro*

  "Hurry! We'll miss the flight!" Luiza Palladio was always in a rush to get somewhere.

  Her brother's powerboat had taken thirty minutes from the Palazzo Palladio on the Grand Canal, passing under the Rialto Bridge, skirting the St. Lucia train station, crossing the Laguna Veneta, and scattering a flock of gulls, to *Aeroporto Marco Polo* Aqua Transport slip on the mainland. Henry James once wrote that Venice is best approached from the sea. The same may be said for the departure.

  "That's my last marathon," Tony said. It seemed to Tony Ferrara that he was always trying to keep up with Luiza. "I can't keep up the pace, Lou."

  "No, no," Luiza said. "Remember, the New York City Marathon is in just two weeks. We're already registered. We have a full two weeks to rest at home. We'll just take it a little easy for a while."

76

Luiza and Tony ran together nearly every day through Central Park, just a few blocks from their high-rise apartment building on West 96th Street. Ten miles on the weekdays and fifteen miles on Saturdays. Sunday was their time to rest, watch a bit of news on the television, and work their way through the *Sunday Times*. After the runs, they would share their two-person *Sunlighten* sauna on the 36th floor of their Upper West Side apartment facing West to the Hudson River.

"We *have* to do the New York. All five boroughs. Start in Staten Island, cross the Verrazano-Narrows Bridge to Brooklyn, brush by the Bronx, cross the Queensboro to Manhattan, up Fifth Avenue to Central Park. Finish at Tavern on the Green, just a ten-minute walk back to the apartment. I get chills just thinking about it."

"I don't know, Lou. Remember last year, we finished in the second half. Fifty-thousand runners, and we finished in the second half."

"We have to go, Tony. Everyone will be there. The reporters will be there. The *Times, Daily News,* even the *Post.* And the glamour magazines. We'll get some great coverage, and that'll be good for business. Let's not forget to remind our photographers."

"I'll be lucky if I can *walk* twenty-six miles by then. Berlin just a couple of weeks ago. Venice this week. I don't know if I'll be able to do the New York, Lou. My muscles aren't like they used to be. It takes them longer to recover. I'm pushing forty, and it feels like I'm *pulling!* Seriously, I'm not sure I can do another one so soon."

"You'll be fine. Your time was good yesterday. Your personal best. You're in great shape."

"I wish that were true," he said.

"You're not getting older, Tony. You're getting better. I bet you'll break your own record in New York. I can just see you now, crossing the finish line in Central Park. A snack at the Tavern on the Green and a short walk home. You'll be wonderful, Darling. Don't worry." She squeezed his hand and kissed him on the cheek, still running on the moving sidewalk to the terminal. "Come on, Darling. We can make it."

"OK, Lou. I'll do it for you. You know I would do anything for you. I always have. You know that. We're a team."

They really were a team. All New York knew it. Luiza had the *panache* and Tony, with his double degree from Penn – Wharton M.B.A. and Law School J.D. – knew the business. Valedictorian at South Philadelphia High School with varsity letters in track and swimming, Tony Ferrara earned a full scholarship to the University of Pennsylvania in West Philly and graduated *summa cum laude* before going on to graduate school, again with a full scholarship to Penn's double-degree program. He loved developing mathematical models for marketing, and that would lead to one of the most successful magazine rollouts in the publishing business.

"We're a good team," she said. "Let's keep running. We can make this flight, and we can do the New York. This time we'll finish in the top half. Wouldn't that be something to write home about! Luiza Palladio and Tony Ferrara, New York's own!"

"I'll get the staff to write a nice piece for the press. With photos. Crossing the finish line. Together."

Luiza and Tony have been together for nearly ten years, both as business partners and as lovers. It's a good match. They work well together, play well together, and run well together. Tony has the good sense to let Luiza take the lead.

Luiza flashed that wide smile that some fifteen years earlier had been featured on the covers of *Cosmopolitan*, *Vogue*, and a dozen other American and international magazines, and now can be seen in the Colgate toothpaste advertisement on the billboard in Times Square. It's the smile that always made Tony a little dizzy. Those bright white teeth. The curl in her lips. How could he ever refuse any of her requests?

From the time Luiza Palladio arrived in Manhattan from Venice as a teenager with a twenty-million-euro inheritance in her *Credit Suisse* bank account, the modeling agencies were all bidding for her services. She had the face that every advertiser wanted. And the figure. While the money was good, she appreciated the attention even more.

Over the years, the modeling jobs gradually declined, so she turned to publishing her own magazine for women of a certain age, *Belle Donne* (Beautiful Women), with makeup tips interleaved with coupons for cosmetics, clothing, and accessories, the latest Milanese fashions, a feature (thanks to Tony) on the law for women in dicey situations – like how to divorce a multimillionaire – and stories of mature women and their loves. "The woman always comes out on top" was her guidance to both contributors and editorial staff.

The magazine, with all its subsidiaries around the world, and translated into twelve languages, has multiplied her net worth. Her earnings from modeling and publishing exceeded her hefty inheritance several times over. Her generally frugal spending habits ensured that the money would not be wasted. She and Tony still took the bus to their office on Park Avenue.

"Don't you love the scenery? That's one of the greatest things about all these marathons. They take you through some of the most beautiful places. Especially the Venice. I always enjoy the Venice. Brings back memories. It's my favorite," Luiza said, still running.

Luiza and Tony were never among the elite runners, never made the racing headlines, but they always finished. Together. Luiza set the pace and Tony kept up. While she seemed to glide along the entire twenty-six miles, he just ground it out, mile after exhausting mile. She wouldn't think of slowing down, and he wouldn't think of dropping out. Or falling behind.

"All the marathons are gorgeous. Tokyo through the Ginza, Boston on Patriot's Day, London finishing at Buckingham Palace. Aren't you glad we did the Berlin last month, starting and finishing at the Brandenburg Gate? The Chicago Loop. They're all great, wonderful races, but the Venice, ah, Venice, *primus inter pares!* First among equals!"

The Venice Marathon started about fifteen miles west of Venice in the small town of Stra on the posh *Riviera del Brenta* and finished in the center of Venice on the edge of the Lagoon in front of the *Arsenale*. Toward the end of the race, runners cross the Grand Canal on a pontoon bridge built in one day for the race.

"I love the last leg of the Venice, don't you? Running past the *Piazza San Marco* and the Doge's Palace, and finishing on the promenade in front of *Giardino Della Marinaressa*, the Mariner's Garden." Of all the marathons Luiza has run around the world, this has always been her favorite.

With all her wealth, Luiza could easily afford a private jet. But she thinks it's a waste of money, and Luiza has never had a wish to waste her money, whether it was inherited or earned on her own. "It takes just as long for a private jet to fly from New York to London as it does for a commercial jet," she often said. She did, however, indulge to the extent of a first-class seat and special treatment at the airports. There was always someone there to greet her.

"He could have gone faster," she said. Her brother is always happy to see his sister, and just as happy to take her back to the airport. It's not that they don't like each other. They really do like each other, but they chose different paths. Luiza couldn't wait to get out of her home town, to see the world, to start her modeling career in New York City. Alessandro chose to stay home. To attend the university in Venice, to become a police officer. In all the years since Luiza left for the Big Apple, they'd become more distant, not only geographically, but emotionally. Luiza has never stopped running, flitting from one project to the next. Sandro doesn't run. He walks. He contemplates. He solves crimes methodically, scientifically. And he's incorruptible.

"They have speed limits. They can't create a wake."

"He's a police officer," she said. "A colonel in the *Carabinieri*. He can create a wake if he wants to."

"Your brother doesn't break the law. He's the real 'Untouchable,' Lou. I wish all police officers were as straight as your brother."

"I suppose you're right. I wouldn't have it any other way. He was always like that. Even as a kid, he was always the straight arrow in the class. Always did his homework. Never talked back. I think he was Mamma's favorite. I'll never know why he chose to be a policeman, but he's certainly been a good one. Well, in any event, let's keep running so we can make this flight," she said.

"I just ran twenty-six miles. I'm all run out, Lou."

"It does seem like another mile to the terminal," she said. "The moving sidewalk will help. Think about it. A twenty-six-mile moving sidewalk. Wouldn't that be something?" she laughed.

"Good thing we packed light," Tony said, shifting his backpack. "We don't have any bags to check. Hope we can get through security fast enough. But I guess that won't be a problem. They see you coming and they whisk you right through. They don't even bother looking at your passport!"

"One of the perks of celebrity, Darling. Everyone knows me – and my brother. They just wave and smile, and I wave and smile back. Sometimes they ask for an autograph. For their daughters, they say. Or their wives. I don't mind. It's good public relations. Home town girl and all that."

"And it also doesn't hurt," Tony added, "when you hand out signed photographs to the immigration and customs officers. And you have no bags to check. You never seem to pack anything when we come to Venice. No clothes or anything."

"I don't need to pack anything when we come to Venice. Everything I need is still at the house."

"The *house*? Is that what you call it? It's a palace. Bigger and better than some of the five-star hotels I've stayed at."

They jumped onto the next segment of the moving walkway and continued to run. A bright autumn morning sun shone through the glass ceiling above the walkway and through the windows facing east, warming the passageway.

"It's a nice house with a nice view of the Grand Canal and the Rialto Bridge, but honestly it's much too big for me," she said. "I prefer our Upper West Side apartment. And it's not New York. Everything is too slow. Slow walkers. Slow talkers. And slow boats!"

"Do you think you'll ever move back? Back home. To Venice?"

"No," she said. "New York is my home. I like the Broadway shows. I like the Yankees. I like the museums. And the concerts at Carnegie Hall."

"They have concerts here in Venice," he said.

"Yes," she said, "there are concerts here every night, but they're all Vivaldi! No, give me the bright lights and the *New York Times* Sunday crossword!"

"You really like New York."

"I *love* New York! What is it Frank Sinatra used to sing? *I want to wake up in a city that never sleeps.*"

"You moved from Venice to New York and your sister-in-law moved from New York to Venice."

"She's nice. Do you like her?"

"I do," he said. "She's a lot like you."

"She's smarter than I am. I'll bet she always did her homework in school. Smarter and tougher. Black belt. Ouch! Don't mess with her."

"I wouldn't dream of it. They're a good match. Ever think of getting married, Luiza? I think *we* would be a good match, don't you?"

"Are you proposing to me, Tony Ferrara? Now? On this moving sidewalk? Running to catch a plane?"

"I suppose I am. Should I get down on one knee?"

"If you can keep running. That'd be a neat trick."

He ran ahead, turned, and dropped to one knee.

"I love you, Luiza Palladio. I have always loved you and I always will. Will you marry me?"

"I love you, too. Yes, Tony Ferrara, I'll marry you. Now get up and keep running! We have another race in two weeks."

PART IV. Winter

Queen of Clouds

Murano

Sunday, December 28, 1986

We feel the chill north winds course through the home
despite the locked and bolted doors...
this is winter, which nonetheless
brings its own delights.
—Antonio Vivaldi, *Inverno, Allegro non molto*

"You've done a nice job with this glass design studio, Sweetheart."

After earning her degree in architecture at *Università Iuav di Venezia,* Angelica Tomlinson designed homes based on the Frank Lloyd Wright model: long, straight lines with no unnecessary adornment. She enjoyed the work – for a while. The pay was good, and her work earned her the Young Architect's Award. But the obsession with straight lines and right angles began to strike her as too repetitive, too confining. She began asking herself if there might be something she could do with more subtlety, allowing for more individuality. She found her answer in the sky: clouds. And she found her medium: glass. And she found her place: Murano, where glass makers have been at work for centuries mastering their craft. She likes the process of turning sand into glass, and she enjoys the smooth feel of the finished product. She set up her offices in the center of the island.

85

"Such a beautiful studio," Ben said. Proud parents, Ben and Fina are enormously pleased with how Angelica had transformed the old building. They supported her when she said she wanted to study architecture, and they supported her when she wanted to make a career change. They helped her to buy the building on Murano and financed the restoration. But the vision was Angelica's. Now Angelica has her own business, and business is good.

"I'm partnering with all the glass factories on the island," she said. "I have the freedom to create my own designs for homes, hotels, and businesses."

"Her work has been featured in a number of art and architectural journals and magazines," David said. "The *Italian Architectural Digest* did a feature on Angelica and her creations. They called her *Regina delle Nuvole*, Queen of Clouds. You should have seen all the mail she received after that issue came out. And the orders. She has commissions for more than two years."

"We have royalty in our family. That's very nice, Your Majesty, but they treat you well?" Fina asked. "These Murano men? They are respectful? If they are not respectful, you let us know. Yes?"

"How would you like being called Queen Mother?" They both laughed. "They treat me well, Mamma. All the men here on the island. We have fun together. I call them 'Uncle,' and they call me 'Little Niece.' They're kind men. And, yes, they're very respectful, Mamma. They always treat me with respect. If an apprentice tries to flirt, his master takes him aside and gives him some advice on how to treat a woman. Then the apprentice comes to me and apologizes. We are a community here. Friendly and professional."

"I'm glad for that," Fina said. "And the pay?" Fina, ever the doting mother, asked. "How is the pay? Do you need anything? Papa and I want to help. If you need anything. Don't be shy."

"The pay is good, Mamma." She pointed to a glass panel, eight feet tall and four feet wide, with a pale blue sky and fluffy white cumulus clouds over a light blue sea. "I just finished that window for a fashion house in Milan. Any idea what they are paying?"

"How much?" Fina asked. "How much are they paying?"

"Sixty thousand euros," Angelica said.

"No! Sixty thousand euros? Truly?"

"Truly, Mamma. And that's not all."

"Her glass clouds are famous, Aunt Fina," David said. "All over the world. She just completed a chandelier for the Sultan of Brunei. Half a million euros." When he wasn't busy with his plans to keep Venice from being swallowed up by the sea, David acted as Angelica's business manager. He was as good with numbers as Angelica was with artistic design. He was the silent partner of *A. Palladio Studio, LLC,* registered as Angelica Palladio Tomlinson, Citizen of Venice. Angelica trusts him without reservation. And she inspires him.

David's office on the third floor of the renovated building is tastefully decorated in Angelica's glass sculptures and colored glass pieces from Murano factories. Even the walls and doors are made of Murano glass using Angelica's designs, as is the ceiling, with its bright white clouds. David never tires of looking up at the puffy cumulus tower cloud above his desk that looks ever so much like a giraffe.

"I always liked clouds," Angelica said. "One could do a scientific study of clouds by visiting the churches and museums in Venice. Those soft clouds in Giovanni Bellini's *Virgin and Child* in the *Museo Correr*. Most visitors look at the mother and the baby. I look at the clouds in the blue sky. Even dark stormy clouds sing to me. Like Jacopo Bellini's *Crucifixion* in the *Correr*. As terrible as that scene is, I can't help but admire the cirrostratus in the background. I think those Venetian artists liked clouds as much as I do. Mamma, you're being quiet."

"Breathtaking," Fina said. "*Bellissimo,* my Angel. Everything you do is so beautiful. And you are so successful. I'm speechless."

"Well, that's a first," Ben said, laughing.

"I'm serious," Fina said. "Everything you do shows your passion. Your *Memorial to the Partisans* brings tears to my eyes. It seems as though you were there. With us. In the mountains."

"It does," Ben said. "It really does seem you were there. With us. All those times you wanted to hear our stories," Ben said. "You were listening. Taking notes."

"And all that time you were spending at the churches," Fina said, "we thought maybe you were becoming religious!"

"No, Mamma, just observing. Religion has caused great harm, but it has also given us some great paintings. Like the Venetian Renaissance."

"Andrea Palladio would be proud, my Angel," Fina said, taking Angelica's hand to her lips. "Very proud. An architect and an artist. Imagine, our daughter, so successful and so happy. You *are* happy, yes?"

"I'm very happy, Mamma. Everything is going well. I'm free to be as creative as I can, and the business is good. I'm just sorry I couldn't give you grandchildren. I guess I've been too wrapped up in my work, in creating art and running a business. There never seems to be time for anything else. I know you would like to have had some little ones running around the *palazzo*."

"No, no, here are my grandchildren, all around us. All these beautiful glass masterpieces. They are much more peaceful. More quiet. And *you* created them. My Angel created them. They are my beautiful grandchildren. No? Isn't that right, my darling? These are your children and my grandchildren."

"Thank you, Mamma. I thought you might be disappointed when I spent so much time at the *Accademia*. I learned a lot in architecture school, but there were too many straight lines, too many right angles. When I looked at the clouds, I saw something else, something softer. That's why I spent so much time in the churches and the museums."

"I understand," Fina said. "you were following your dream. Isn't that right, Benjy? Benjy?"

"Oh, I was just thinking about David," Ben said. "David, how are you coming with your plan to save Venice from the sea?"

"I've looked at all the proposals," David said. "They're all short-term solutions. Twenty years at most. We should be looking at the next *hundred* years. *Two* hundred."

"And your solution?"

"Give Venice back to the sea."

"You've given up?" Fina asked. "A brilliant civil engineer from MIT, and you're giving up?"

"No, Aunt Fina, I'm not giving up. I've just abandoned the short-term solutions. Yes, we can replace old bricks with new and stronger bricks. We can dredge the canals every few years. That would make room for more water to flow through the city. We can build floodgates and install pumps. We can raise the walkways, like we do every time high water floods the city. We can build breakwaters out in the Lagoon to slow the rush of the waves, and we can even change the shapes of the shorelines. We can do all these things, and we will have to do them, but these are all like trying to empty the ocean with a teaspoon. We've been burning fossil fuels for generations, and now all that oil and coal and gas is finally giving us the bill. Payment is due."

"I agree with David," Ben said. "Those are all short-term fixes, and we'll do them until we can do something more permanent. We should focus our efforts on the long term. What are you thinking, David?"

"My proposal is to build a New Venice," David said.

"A new Venice? Where?" Fina asked. "How is that possible?"

"Yes, a New Venice, *Nuova Venezia*. And where? We build New Venice right on top of today's Venice."

"How long would it take, this *Nuova Venezia* of yours?" Fina asked.

"It'll take fifty to a hundred years or more, but in those years, we can build, block by block, three meters above the current city."

"Three meters?" Fina asked. "It sounds strange, David. But why three meters? We would need lots of steps to get up to the New Venice? So why does it have to be so much?"

"The sea is rising, Aunt Fina. Rising faster than anyone ever imagined. The polar ice caps are melting. They'll continue to melt until they're completely gone, and all the melted ice will go into the sea. The sea will continue to rise. I've calculated with a high probability that the water will rise two meters in the next hundred years, maybe up to three meters in some forecasts. We can't save everything. Some treasures will be gone. We can't lift the Doge's Palace or the Basilica, and the Piazza San Marco will be under at least two meters of water permanently, but we can save much of the city if we have the will."

"That sounds expensive," Fina said.

"It'll be more expensive the longer we wait," David said. "We can start now to build a trust fund. It will take billions. I've spoken to people at UNESCO, the banks, and the merchants' organizations, as well as the church. Most are so short-sighted they can't see what's right before their eyes. But there are a few who see clearly enough. We can do it."

"Fina and I have some influence," Ben said. "And some money. I'll put in the seed money provided *you* are the project manager."

"I appreciate your confidence, Uncle Ben, but I won't be able to work much longer."

"Why? What's wrong?"

"I'm sick," he said.

"What do you mean, sick? We'll get the best doctors."

"I've been to the doctors. They all say the same thing."

"They can do nothing?" Fina asked.

"Nothing."

91

"Tell them, David," Angelica said.

"It's something called human immunodeficiency virus and acquired immune deficiency syndrome," David said. "HIV AIDS. And it's incurable. The good news is I won't be around to see Venice flooded," he laughed.

"Oh, David," Fina said. "Don't joke. You're not going to die."

"I'm already dead, Aunt Fina."

Ben put his arms around David and kissed him on the cheek. "If Lazarus could be brought back from the dead, you can, too. I know some people in New York. The best doctors in the world. On the leading edge. We'll go to New York. They'll see me."

"It's no good," David said. "All the money and influence in the world can't stop this thing."

"David, I've never known you to give up," Ben said. "You haven't given up on saving Venice from being swallowed up by the sea. You used your mind, your imagination, to think of new ways of solving the problem."

"This problem is outside my sphere of knowledge," David said. "I don't know medicine. I don't know what this thing is. All I know is that lots of people are dying from it."

"I don't know much about medicine," Angelica said, "but Papa has a friend in New York who does. Papa, you've talked about your college roommate. Remember?"

"Ben," Fina said, "the man we met in Brooklyn all those years ago. What was his name?"

"Victor. Victor Poulos. That's right. Vic was a physics major. He went on to medical school at Harvard and got his M.D. and his Ph.D. in medical research. He founded a company that's doing some remarkable work."

"David, this man was *Time* magazine's Man of the Year," Angelica said. "I remember the article. His company is doing research in diseases that many people thought were incurable. The article said he was an optimist. He said there is no disease we cannot defeat. He can help you. Don't give up hope, Cousin."

"This man, he can help David come back to life," Fina said.

"David," Angelica said, "Do you remember the time we first met, in front of the Danieli? I told you to look up. What did you see?"

"A giraffe?"

"Look up at the sky now," she said. "What do you see? Do you know what I see? Hope! That's what I see."

"Pack your bag, my dear Lazarus," Ben said. "We're going to New York."

I am the daughter of earth and water,
  And the nursling of the sky.
    —From *The Cloud,* by Percy Bysshe Shelley

Farewell, My Hero

Cimiterio di San Michele, Isola di San Michele

Friday, February 16, 2007

To rest contentedly beside the hearth, while those outside are drenched by pouring rain.
—Antonio Vivaldi, *Inverno, Largo*

"My Esperanza," he whispered. "They never knew." He knelt in the rain by the white marble stone.

Esperanza Maria Grosso De Franceschi di Venezia
1925-2007
Beloved wife and mother
Hero of the Resistance

"They never knew. They have never known what you did during the war. And maybe they wouldn't believe. But I must tell them. Before it's too late. They must know your story. My Esperanza. My Hope. My brave girl." His eyes filled with tears as he recalled the first time he saw her.

"What are you doing here? This is no job for a girl."

"Oh, and can you ride your bicycle past the German guards with a wink and a smile? No? I didn't think so."

"Oh, what do we have here? A sassy one. Well, we'll find out how sassy you are. Who sent you? How did you find us? Where did you come from?"

"You have nice eyes," the girl said.

"Never mind that. Just answer the questions. How do we know you're not a spy? You look like a spy to me. Doesn't she look like a spy, fellows?"

Partisan bands were constantly being infiltrated by Mussolini's Fascists and Hitler's Nazis. The infiltrators came in all shapes and sizes. One could never be too careful.

"You ask a lot of questions," the tiny but confident 18-year-old Esperanza Grosso said. "All right, I guess you have to ask questions so you won't shoot me with that stick you're holding. So, I'll tell you. First, 'My Friend' sent me. You know 'My Friend,' *si?*"

"Never mind that. His code name?"

"You know him as *Il Falco, si?* He told me where to find you."

"Go on."

"OK, *Compagno*, but please put your gun away. You won't need it, and it might go off by accident."

"If it goes off, it won't be by accident."

"I come from *Sestieri Dorsoduro*. In Venice. My house is on the *Campo San Trovaso*. That's my neighborhood. On the south side of the *Rio del Ognisanti*. I was born and raised in the same neighborhood. Lived there all my life. You want to know the name of my first-grade teacher?"

"What church?"

"What church? What kind of question is that? Well, I don't do church anymore, but I was baptized in *Chiesa di San Trovaso*, if you must know. You know Venice?"

"I know Venice. What else?"

"The water will be more than one meter high in the *Piazza San Marco* this spring."

95

"She's all right. She knows the password. What's your name?"

"Esperanza Grosso. You can call me *L'Airone*."

"Heron, eh? Skinny. Long neck. Like a heron. I'm Gianni De Franceschi. You can call me *Sir*," he said with a smile.

"I'll call you *Smug*, if you don't mind."

The others laughed. "Smug. That's a good one, little bird. So now down to business. You know who we are. It's dangerous work. What are your orders? From *Il Falco*."

"My orders are to follow your orders," she said. "And take my bicycle. That's all. he says you're a good leader. I trust him. So, I trust you. That's all. *È tutto*."

"Thanks for the compliment. All right. So far," he said, "we've derailed two supply trains, and we're the ones who blew up the petrol tank in Padua. We picked off a bunch of Nazi officers. And none of our band killed or wounded. First rule, *Airone*. No casualties. I heard something the American general Patton said. 'I don't want to die for my country. I want the other guy to die for *his* country.' That's what he said. Something like that."

"It's a good philosophy," she said. "I don't want to die for Venice. I want the Nazi pigs to die for Hitler. So, what do you want me to do?"

"*La mia cara ragazza*, my darling Essie," Gianni whispered, with his hand on the marble stone. "So young. So trusting. I fell in love with you from the moment I saw you. You called me 'Smug,' and I laughed. Do you remember? I remember, Sweetheart. I remember like it was yesterday. Every word you spoke made me love you more."

It was Gianni's lucky day, that day when Esperanza Grosso came into his camp, riding her bicycle. Fearless. Ready to do her part in the Resistance. It was that memory that gave him comfort through all the years.

"Sixty-four years we were together. In all that time, I never stopped loving you. So smart. So young. Just eighteen years old. So brave. When the war was over, and we got married, I promised to take care of you. Remember? But you took care of me all those years. How did you put up with me? My aches and pains and complaints. Sometimes you seemed more like a nurse, my own special nurse."

"You didn't complain much, Essie, although I wouldn't have minded if you complained now and then. Now that I think about it, you *never* complained. In all those years. I said, if you live to be a hundred, I want to die one day before, because I never wanted to be apart from you. You survived the guns and the grenades. You survived the war. But that enemy we never saw, that cancer…we never saw it coming."

"We need to know the layout of the German station at Vigonza. We need to find out what's going on at that place. American and British intelligence indicates not many troops there, but it seems like there's always a large number of high-ranking German officers being chauffeured in and out on a regular basis. Our mission is to find out what's going on there and report back to the Italian Committee for National Liberation, the CLN. What they'll do with the intelligence I can only guess. Maybe take prisoners, or maybe bomb it. First we need to find out what all those high-ranking officers are doing there."

"Vigonza. It's not far."

"We need someone on the inside. Can you help?"

"I can help. I have a suggestion. I'm a good cook. All kinds of pasta. And baking. It's my specialty. My mother taught me some tricks in baking bread and cakes. I know how to make them look delicious, and smell delicious, and taste delicious. I'll take some to the base and tell them I'm looking for a job. I'll wear my schoolgirl uniform. And I'll smile ever so sweetly. After they smell my breads and taste my cakes, I'm sure they'll hire me. How could they resist!"

He caressed the cool headstone. The violets in front of the stone will soon add their bright purple to the place.

"That's what you did, my Little Heron. You baked some delicious breads and cakes and cookies, and you rode your bicycle right up to the gate, right up to the sentries. You smiled that big smile of yours and opened the box so they could see and smell. 'Have some,' you said. They let you pass and you went straight to the Commandant's office. You knocked on the door and walked right in carrying your breads and cakes and cookies. I couldn't believe it when you told the guys in our group."

"None of them could believe what you did that day. You just marched right up to the Commandant! You took him by surprise. Such bravery. Who could do such a thing? I always said you should have been an actress. Didn't I say that, *Cara mia*? Didn't I always say you should be on the stage? Or in the cinema? Oh! All the boys would have been upside down. Esperanza, the famous actress! So beautiful. So slender you were. Long, thin legs. Like the herons in the Lagoon. So graceful. So pretty. So innocent."

"You've been working in the kitchen for a week. I'm glad to see you're all right. They didn't hurt you? What did you find out? What's the layout? What's going on in that place? Why do so many German officers go in and out? Tell me."

"I'm fine. They didn't hurt me. They suspected nothing. I found out it's a communications station. All the men there are speaking German and Italian, but also English and Russian, if I'm not mistaken. It sounds like they're intercepting radio messages in all those languages and translating them into German. The women in the kitchen. They gossip all the time."

"They gossip? What do they gossip about?"

"About everything. They don't like Mussolini, but they pretend they like him. They make jokes about Hitler, but not when they can be overheard. I notice things, but I keep my head down. They treat me like a little girl, their helper."

"And soldiers?"

"There are soldiers with rifles in each of the buildings. They just walk around with their rifles slung over their shoulders. They're just kids playing a game. I don't think they would ever have the nerve to shoot anyone."

"How about the layout? The physical layout. The buildings? How many are there? How big. What do they look like?"

"It's simple. Here, I'll draw it for you. Four buildings around a square. Each building is twenty meters long and five meters wide. No windows in any of the buildings. Only one level. On the south side, there's a privy."

She drew a diagram on a scrap of paper.

"On the north side of the square is the office of the Commandant and his staff. All paperwork. On the east side is the dining hall and the kitchen, where I work. There's another privy behind the kitchen. On the other two sides, it looks like that's where the real work is done. Antennas on the roof covered with canvas. Machines inside. They look like typewriters, but bigger than regular typewriters. They have different keyboards from regular typewriters."

"Coding machines. Enigma. It's their secret coding device. They think it's unbreakable, but *I* have no doubt the Americans and the British can break it."

"The men at the machines jump up and give their papers to a sergeant sitting at a desk at the front of the room. Sometimes the sergeant picks up the telephone and speaks to someone higher up."

"Higher up? How do you know?"

"I can tell because the sergeant clicks his heels and stands to attention. It's rather funny. And the tone of his voice. It's more deferential when he's talking on the telephone. I can pick up a few words of the German, like when he finishes his telephone conversation, he always salutes with his arm up and shouts, 'Heil Hitler.' Always the same."

"How do you know all this? It's good intelligence, but how do you do it? They let you inside?"

"I bring cakes and cookies and coffee and tea at ten o'clock in the morning. And again, at four o'clock in the afternoon. I smile and hand out the treats. They all stop work when I come in. They all smile at me and thank me. So polite."

"You look so innocent. Nobody suspects anything."

"I don't look around. I just smile at the soldiers and hand out the treats."

"Don't they try to make conversation?"

"They try, but I look away. '*Io non parlo tedesco.*' I don't speak German. The sergeant keeps them in line."

"What else? How about the security?"

"I don't know much about fortifications, but that place doesn't seem secure. They have one watch tower, but there are trees and shrubs all around. One other thing. These German soldiers. They don't seem much like soldiers. They seem more like school boys. They don't even shave!"

"Well done! You've done a good job. This is excellent intelligence, *l'Airone*. We'll get this to the Allies. They'll know what to do with it. Now that's done, let's see what happens next. What you did, Little Heron, going in like that, it took a lot of nerve. It was your plan, and you pulled it off. You'll get a medal."

"When the attack came, the entire compound was obliterated. All thanks to you, *Cara mia*. The King wanted to give us all medals. But you didn't want a medal. You didn't want to be famous. You just wanted to come home to Venice, to a normal life. Still not yet twenty years old."

Historians have estimated that some 50,000 Italian partisans were killed, wounded, or captured during World War II. Many were young men and women, still in their teens.

"When our band was breaking up, I couldn't bear the thought that I might never see you again. I ran in front of your bicycle as you were leaving. You almost ran me down. You stopped."

101

"*L'Airone*, please don't go. I love you with all my heart." You were still sitting on your bicycle and I dropped to one knee. "I know I'm not rich or handsome, but I promise I will love you and I will take care of you all my life. And I will do my best to make you happy."

"What are you doing, Smug?"

"What do you think? I'm asking you to marry me."

He kissed the headstone and pressed his cheek to the cool marble.

"Now I must go. I'll be back tomorrow, Sweetheart. I must write your stories. You fought so bravely with the Resistance until the end. We beat them, my dearest Esperanza. My dearest Essie. My Hope. *Esperanza di La Serenissima. Abbiamo vinto la vittoria!* We won the victory! Now, sleep my love. Sleep."

La Donna Partigiana - a monument to the women killed fighting as partisans in World War II that is only visible at low tide.

A Police Story

December, 2015

1. *Palazzo Cavalli.*

We tread the icy path slowly and cautiously, for fear of tripping and falling.
Then turn abruptly, slip, crash on the ground and, rising, hasten on across the ice lest it cracks up.
We feel the chill north winds course through the home despite the locked and bolted doors...
this is winter, which nonetheless brings its own delights.
—Antonio Vivaldi, *Inverno, Allegro*

"Gabriela," she announced. "Gabriela Sofia Nadal-Martin. From New York City."

He smiled. He took her hand and kissed it. "Alessandro," he said. "My name is Alessandro Palladio. From right here, in Venice."

He held her hand. She didn't mind.

"You were expecting me? You got the fax?"

He kissed her hand again and returned it to the slightly built, dark-haired young woman.

"We did. Not only that, but I received a call from your Governor. When he was a Rhodes Scholar at Oxford, we were on the Christ Church rugby team. We've managed to keep in touch. We certainly have been expecting you. Three months? You're on loan to us for three months?"

"The Governor thinks we can wrap it up by then."

"Wrap it up?"

"Either catch the guy or give up."

"Give up?"

"No, I mean catch him or …."

"I know what you mean," he said. "Let's do the first. Before the 'or.' Let's catch him."

She nodded her agreement. "I'm only budgeted for three months. They're giving me a living allowance of a hundred dollars a day plus air fare. Ten thousand total."

He managed to suppress a smile. He tried to look serious. "A hundred dollars a day. Ten thousand total."

"That's what the accountants figured it would take."

He could contain himself no more. "Please forgive me," he said with a broad smile.

She didn't think she had ever been in the presence of such a handsome man. Tall. Dark. And really handsome. "Why? You think it's too much?"

"Gabriela Sofia Nadal-Martin From New York City, someone is playing a joke on you."

"Sir, this is not a joking matter," she said. "This man has killed six women in New York, and it looks like he has relocated here, to Venice, and I've been tracking him for three years."

"Please, *Signorina*, I beg your forgiveness. Of course, it is no joking matter. Of course. I only meant to say…."

"What?" she said.

"I don't know what you can do here for a hundred dollars a day. Maybe a cheap hostel, where the college boys and girls stay, and a bit of lasagna once a day. That's about what a hundred dollars will get you. Ten thousand total? Over Christmas and New Year's? Ten thousand will last you about six weeks. At the most."

"They said it would be no problem this time of year. They said the tourists come in the spring and summer. They said nobody goes to Venice in the winter."

"Ah, my dear, *they* are mistaken."

"Well, I want to get to work on the case, but I have to find a place to stay."

"You know what they say here?"

"What?"

"They say, *Hakuna Matata!*"

"That's not Italian. That's Swahili. It's a song from *The Lion King*. I've seen it on Broadway three times."

"We say it here, too, but we also say, *Nessun problema*, no problem."

"No problem? I have a hundred dollars a day, and you say I have to live with a bunch of college kids on semester break?"

"I wouldn't dream of it. You'll stay with me."

"With *you?* I don't know what you heard about me, Mister, but…."

"No buts," he said. "I spoke with your Governor. He says you are – how did he put it? – 'the sharpest tack in the box.' Valedictorian, Hunter College High School, bachelor's degree summa cum laude in psychology from Hunter College, NYU Law Review, turned down six-figure salary with a big Wall Street law firm to become an Assistant District Attorney for New York County – and incorruptible. Or should I say *Untouchable?* And you teach self-defense courses at the 92nd Street Y."

"You left out my birthday."

"January 21, 1977. Born in Spanish Harlem, oldest of three children, one brother, one sister."

105

"I don't believe this!"

"Your mother and your father came from Puerto Rico. Your father, Julio Nadal, is an automobile mechanic, and your mother, Valentina Martin is a seamstress."

"Is there anything you don't know about me?"

"I don't know if you prefer spaghetti Bolognese or marinara."

"Both. My parents are Puerto Rican but my godmother is Italian. And a wonderful cook."

"Where is your luggage?"

"Right here. My backpack and this carry-on."

"You're joking!"

"No, this is it. I got an appointment as a temporary Federal Air Marshal, so I have my ammunition and cleaning gear in my backpack."

"And your weapon?"

She reached behind her waist and pulled out a black 9 millimeter Glock and held it flat in the palm of her hand. "Qualified expert," she said.

"*Stupefacente!*" he exclaimed. "Amazing!"

"So, seriously, Inspector, where am I going to hang my hat tonight?"

"You have a hat?"

"Figure of speech."

"Well, ADA Nadal-Martin, come with me. We will find the place to hang your hat – so to speak."

They walked down the marble staircase to the ground floor and out the door to face the Grand Canal. A sleek bronze-colored water taxi was moving from left to right toward the Rialto Bridge, passing a vaporetto headed in the opposite direction toward the *Piazza San Marco*.

106

A gondola was bobbing over the wake of the power boats. The gondolier stood, shifting his weight from foot to foot to maintain his balance, while the passengers were busy posing with their cameras looking for the best shots of the Rialto Bridge and the boat traffic on the Grand Canal.

"I know something about you, Inspector."

"All good, I hope."

"According to my sources, you come from an old Venetian family. One of your ancestors was the famous architect, Andrea Palladio. His designs are famous and still used all over the world."

"A great man. He made his mark."

"You went to Eton and Oxford. You rowed on the Christ Church crew and played rugby – with our Governor – and soccer."

"Football, if you please."

"You have no interest in politics. You're officially an Inspector with the rank of Colonel in the *Carabinieri*, the youngest colonel in the service. Incorruptible but a cause of constant irritation to your superiors. That's why you have your office here by the Rialto Bridge rather than in the *Carabinieri* headquarters in the *Piazza San Marco*."

"Ouch! But that's pretty much it. Anything else you want to know?"

"As a matter of fact, yes. Where are we going?"

"We're already here. Welcome to *Palazzo Palladio*!"

"This is your home? A palace?"

"Be it ever so humble…."

"Ah, yes, I forgot. Your sister is the publisher of a New York fashion magazine, and you just happen to be one of the richest men in all of Italy."

"It's true about my sister. You have but to look in the closets in our house. Luiza keeps her Milanese wardrobe just in case she pops in, as she does from time to time. As for the money, just rumors. I give away my entire salary to people who need it more than I do."

That surprised Gabriela. "Your *entire* salary? You give away all of your salary."

"All of it," he said. "Look, Venice is a rich city. It's been rich for centuries. But the people who work here, they're not rich. They can't even afford to live in the city. They live in Mestre or even farther away. I don't need the money. They do."

"You give it to the church?"

"Not to the church," he said. "The church has more than enough money. The priests live well. They have food and housing. I give it to the people directly. No overhead."

Gabriela smiled. This is a man she could like – a lot.

"According to the magazines, you're one of the nation's most eligible bachelors. And a viscount, no less."

"You make me blush. I have never understood the term 'eligible bachelor.' As for the title of viscount, it has been passed down from a much earlier generation. I did nothing to earn it. One of my ancestors earned it by doing something nice for the King. But do come in."

He removed a small device from his pocket and pressed a button. The front door opened wide. *"Benvenuto in casa mia!* Welcome to my house!"

As they walked through the door and entered a wide entry hall with bright white marble floors, Gabriela noticed a large library on the left. The shelves were full, up to the ceiling. A mahogany ladder stood against the wall.

Alessandro led the way past several other rooms that appeared to be furnished with leather sofas and chairs and into the dining hall. The table appeared to be polished walnut and could seat twelve. They continued into the kitchen.

"This kitchen is extraordinary," she said. "It's larger than my family's entire apartment in New York. Your cook must have roller skates to get around!"

"It happens, my dear lady, that *I* am the cook," Alessandro said. "And I do not use roller skates."

"You do your own cooking?"

"Indeed, I am a cook," he said, "and I think a cook of some competence, if I may say so, and I do my own shopping. Cooking is one of my passions. And shopping assures me that I have only the freshest fruits and vegetables, and fish and meats."

"That's not the only reason you do your own grocery shopping, surely," she said.

"True enough. It also allows me to move around the city without causing any disruption. My neighbors are accustomed to seeing me in the *Mercato di Rialto* and in the supermarket just along the street here. I can stop for conversation. You can imagine the information I receive every day walking through the market."

A quick look at the pantry behind the kitchen left Gabriela wide-eyed. It must have been at least six meters on each side. There were cabinets from floor to ceiling, each with a small neatly printed sign indicating its contents. The entire area was spotless with a slight scent of lemon.

"From the looks of the pantry, it looks like you do quite a bit of shopping," she said.

"We'll go to your room now," Alessandro said, as he led the way to a polished mahogany staircase. At the top of the stairs, he turned to her and said, "You have your choice. There are three suites on this floor and another three on the next level. Two of the suites upstairs are being held for my sister, but she seldom uses them, perhaps once every year or two. This is my room." He opened the door to a magnificent suite with large windows overlooking the Grand Canal. There was a four-poster bed neatly made up. "The other suites on this level have not such a view, but they are quite comfortable."

"I can only imagine," the astonished Gabriela said. She had once attended a cocktail party at the Plaza Hotel in New York City in a suite that was less spacious and less luxurious than the one in which she now found herself.

"If you want this view, you will have to go to the next level. The suites there are exactly the same as those on this floor. Each suite has its own bath and shower. What do you think? Do you want one of the suites on this level or the Canal view upstairs?"

"Wait just a minute," she said. "You're suggesting that I stay here with you in your palazzo?"

"Suggesting? No. Insisting. You have freedom here. Come and go as you like. I only propose one thing."

"And that one thing?"

"We take turns preparing the main meal. I'll do the dinner tonight and you'll take charge tomorrow."

"Nothing else?" she asked.

"Nothing else."

"And the rent? How much will you be charging? I'm not at all certain I can afford the rent for such a suite."

"Rent? What rent? Please. You embarrass me. You are my guest. Stay for as long as you like. If you find at any time you want to move to another place, feel free. But I think you'll find a hundred dollars a day will consign you to a poor situation. We will have a much better partnership if you are comfortable. *Sì?*"

"Nothing more? I mean...."

"My dear, I know precisely what you mean. And, no," he said, "nothing more. It will be my honor to host the distinguished Assistant District Attorney for the County of New York."

"You know, Inspector, I have a black belt in *karate*."

"Indeed, I'm quite aware of that fact. Well, your skill in martial arts may serve us well as we track down this monster."

"All right," she said, holding out her hand. "It will be my pleasure to accept your kind offer of hospitality. And for my first meal, I shall make for you a nice *arroz con dulce!*" This time, Alessandro shook it and they sealed the bargain.

2. The Venice Jazz Club
Dorsoduro, *Ponte dei Pugni*

"That was great, Sandro. Just a little hesitation on the down beat," Federico said with a smile.

Federico Ferro not only owns The Venice Jazz Club, but he is also the leader of the famous VJC Quartet and is its principal pianist, as well as its genial host and resident wit.

Alessandro laughed and shook Federico's hand. "I'll try harder next time."

"Don't worry. I think everybody in the audience enjoyed it. Especially *Georgia on My Mind.* That was sweet. Mellow. I heard a gentleman over there in the corner say he thought you were the second-best jazz pianist in the house tonight."

The Venice Jazz Club is tucked neatly behind the *Ponte dei Pugni* on the *Fondamenta del Squero* on the *Rio di San Barnaba* in the *sestiere* of Dorsoduro, around the corner from *Campo Santa Margherita* near the University of Venice. Three small open barges are tied up at the opposite side of the canal, their decks filled with bright red, yellow, and green fruits and vegetables from farms near and far. It's not so much the vendors on the barges, or the shoppers at the stores along the canal, who enter the doors of the renowned Venice Jazz Club. It's the local Venetian jazz aficionados and visitors from around the world who have heard from their friends and read in the travel columns of their local newspapers about this unique place and its outstanding musicians. "If you go to Venice," the travel writers advise, "you must find your way to the great Venice Jazz Club. It's the place to be."

"Second best pianist?" Alessandro said. "Well, that's quite a compliment coming from such a well-informed and discerning audience as you have here at this esteemed venue. I'm flattered. I really am. But if I'm the second best, who, pray tell, might be the first? I would certainly like to meet such a person."

"Ah, modesty does not permit, my dear friend. Keep practicing and, who knows, maybe one day. What is it they say, 'How do you get to the Venice Jazz Club? Practice, practice, practice!' But seriously, Sandro, thanks for sitting in. You know you're always welcome here – provided you come for pleasure and not on police business. Not that we have anything to hide. We're a respectable law-abiding business here. No drugs. No guns. No alcohol. What am I saying? Of course, there is a modest amount of stimulating beverages on offer. Surely, the most honorable *Carabinieri* wouldn't deny our customers a glass of refreshing Venetian *Prosecco Spumante?*"

"It was fun," Alessandro said. "Sitting in with you and your band. But I must tell you, it's a little intimidating to be playing a set with these incredible musicians. I feel like I'm crashing a party of professionals."

"Not to worry, my friend. You did fine."

"It was a sellout crowd," Alessandro said. "You must be doing well with the Club."

"You want to know a secret, Sandro? About this business?

"I'm all ears."

"Then let me ask you a question. How does a jazz musician end up with one million euros? Can you tell me that?"

113

"I don't know. Tell me. How does a jazz musician end up with one million euros?"

"By starting with *two* million euros!"

Alessandro groaned. Gabriela laughed.

"Do you know the difference between a jazz musician and an extra-large pizza?" Federico was on a roll.

"No. Tell me, Fedo. What's the difference between a jazz musician and an extra-large pizza?"

"The pizza can feed a family of four!"

More groans and laughs.

"Do you know the difference between a rock guitarist and a jazz guitarist?" Federico asked. "Here's a hint. It's a mathematics problem."

"A mathematics problem?" Sandro asked.

"Yes. You see, the rock guitarist plays 3 chords for 1,000 people, and the jazz guitarist plays 1,000 chords for 3 people."

"Very funny," Alessandro said. "I've missed your terrible jokes."

"Hey, Sandro, one more joke."

"OK, one more joke."

"Two musicians and a drummer walk into a bar."

"Oh, that's cold!"

"I couldn't resist."

"I apologize for being away so long," Alessandro said. "You have such a wonderful club here. The food's good, what there is of it."

"Ah, we are not a restaurant. Read the sign."

"And the guys. I love your quartet. And despite your cruel last joke, the percussion is excellent, and the guitar, and the bass."

"It's the best jazz band in the whole of Italy," Federico said.

"And, of course," Alessandro said, "I will admit, reluctantly, you are *the* best pianist in the house. I'll go so far to say the best jazz pianist in Venice."

"Thank you, my friend. I appreciate your honest assessment of our humble band. We'd like to see more of you in the Club – but not on business."

"You have my word. I promise I'll come more often in the future."

"And your guest, Sandro? The fair Gabriela. My dear *Signorina* Gabriela, how did you like the performance tonight?" Federico asked. "What's your critical assessment, from the point of view of a sophisticated New York jazz connoisseur? Did we measure up to the standard of the Big Apple?"

"For sure. You guys are terrific," Gabriela said. "I agree with Alessandro. Absolutely first-rate. World class. I knew Venice was the home of Vivaldi, but the Venice Jazz Club, as well. *Fantastico!* Reminds me of The Blue Note in Manhattan. Have you been there?"

"I have not had that pleasure. Are you inviting me? Be careful. I would be eager to accept."

"I'm inviting you. You'll be my guest," Gabriela said. "Any time you can get away from this incredible city, you come to *my* city, New York, and I'll take you to the Blue Note."

"And Birdland? I hear from a few of our customers who know about New York City that Birdland might be a good place to hear some of the best jazz musicians in the world."

"You heard right. There's Birdland, The Blue Note, Iridium, Jazz Standard, Dizzy's Smoke. I especially like the Village Vanguard on 7th Avenue in Greenwich Village. You'd like it, too. They have the best jazz musicians in the world. I'll be sure to get us a really good table up front. There are so many places to hear great jazz in New York. Nothing quite so intimate as you have here, but we can keep you busy getting around to all the jazz clubs."

"So, it seems you like jazz."

"*Mi piace il jazz molto*," she said.

"Such good Italian," Federico said to Alessandro. "Such talent."

"This young lady has many talents," Alessandro said. "She's been learning Italian. She's a quick study."

"I hear just a little trace of an accent," Federico said. "What could it be? Let me see? Spanish, maybe? French? No, I think maybe *Español?*"

"Maybe," Gabriela said. "Maybe Puerto Rican?"

"No, not Puerto Rican," he said.

Gabriela had always deluded herself thinking that she had no accent. But she knew better. "Not Puerto Rican?" she said. "Are you sure?"

"*Si*, maybe some Puerto Rican," Federico said. "How do you say it? *Nuyorican?*" He laughed and shook her hand. "I know some incredible jazz musicians from Puerto Rico. Some of the best in the business. You know, of course, the great José Feliciano. And you know David Sánchez on sax? Eddie Gómez on bass? Fantastic musicians. I'll invite them. We'll have Puerto Rico Celebration Night. So, *Señorita Nuyorican*, you're welcome any time to our Club – and you don't need to bring this guy!"

All the patrons had finished their drinks and paid their tabs. A party of Norwegian and Swedish tourists gathered at the bar to buy the Quartet's CDs and the famous *JVC* T-shirts. It had been a full house, as it usually is, but the happy patrons filed out quickly through the front door, spilling out onto the *Fondamenta del Squero* along the small canal, the *Rio di San Barnaba*, connecting with the Grand Canal and the *Ca' Rezzonico* vaporetto stop a few hundred meters from the Club.

The musicians – except for the percussionist, who just picked up his sticks – packed their instruments into velvet lined cases and closed the snaps. The trumpeter had two cases, one for the E-flat trumpet and another for the smaller B-flat cornet. They shook hands with the few remaining customers as they were passing the bandstand, then left through the front door, following the line of customers, and lighting their cigarettes as soon as they were outside on the sidewalk.

The serving staff cleared and wiped the tables. The kitchen staff washed and dried the pots and pans and the plates and utensils. When they were finished, they all left with waves and *Buona notte.*

The place was now empty except for Federico, Alessandro, and Gabriela. Federico locked and bolted the front door and turned off the lights in the hallway and restrooms. Only one dim table lamp remained, sitting on a shelf above the refrigerator in the tiny kitchen.

"Let's go in the back," Federico whispered. "In the kitchen. There are no windows. I think we should keep our voices down. What is it they say? The walls have ears?"

They moved through the darkened room, past the tables, and into the small kitchen. Federico drew the curtain between the dining room and the kitchen. They sat around the work table on wooden chairs. Federico poured three glasses of sparkling *Prosecco di Conegliano spumante*. "Sandro, do you have any idea how you get a jazz musician off your front porch?

"I don't know, Fedo. How do you get a jazz musician off your front porch?"

"Pay for the pizza!"

"Very funny." Sandro wasn't laughing.

"I know what you want, Sandro, my friend. This is dangerous business, you know. We're not dealing with a small-time hood. This is serious. Not like my jokes. This is serious."

"I know, Fedo," Alessandro said softly. "This maniac has killed six young women in New York. After the sixth victim, the killings stopped. Then a month later, they started again, this time in Venice. So far, four young women have been killed here in Venice. It's the same pattern. We're sure he aims to kill two more here before he's done. We're on his trail. We need to catch this monster. Gabriela knows the whole story. Let her tell you."

"I've been on this case for three years," Gabriela said. "I know this man. I've profiled him. I know he's a big man, with big hands. He sneaks up on his victims from behind and strangles them with his bare hands. He must be big and he must be strong, and I'm certain he's here, in Venice, now."

"You've been tracking this big man for three years. And you know for certain he's an American?" Federico asked.

"There's no evidence to the contrary," Gabriela said. "He fits the white anti-Semitic profile. We know the type, and they're Americans. I'm sure there are men like this in other countries, but we're very sure he's an American. Most likely a member of some hate group."

"And he kills women? This American? He must be a coward. To sneak up behind a woman like that. Young women? Only a coward would do such a thing."

"His victims are all young Jewish women. He always kills on Friday nights. In synagogues. We believe he'll strike this Friday or a Friday in the next few weeks. At or near one of the synagogues in Venice."

"You're certain he's an American? A big man? With big hands? If you could see such a man, maybe you could recognize him? This big coward?"

"You *know* something, Fedo," Alessandro said. "What is it? What can you tell us? Anything. We need to find this man. Soon."

"Big man," Federico said. "I think I may know such a man. A big man. Almost two meters tall. Heavy. Very heavy man. Seems like an American. No foreign accent. And I'm pretty good at hearing accents."

"You've seen this man, Federico?" Gabriela asked.

"I think so. I think I may have seen such a man. I've talked to him a few times. He sounds like an American. No accent. Says he's a freelance journalist. He likes jazz. He likes that we're all white men! Doesn't want to hear about Louis Armstrong. Or Ella Fitzgerald. Anybody black. Or female."

"Sounds about right," Gabriela said.

"It sounds really strange," Federico said. "For someone who says he likes jazz but doesn't like Louis or Ella. Strange. He's been coming in every Saturday night. One time, he let slip that he came to follow the story of the murders. But something's not right."

"What else, Fedo? What's not right? What can you tell us? No jokes, Fedo. No more jokes. Not now. This is no time for jokes."

"How can a man like jazz and not like Louis or Ella? Not like anybody who's black or female? What kind of man is that?"

"Fedo, you said something's not right," Alessandro said. "What did you mean? What's not right?"

"If you know something," Gabriela said, "please tell us. It could be important."

"Well, the thing is…"

"What?" Alessandro asked.

"Well, the thing is, he arrived in Venice a week before the first synagogue murder. So how is he following the story before it happens?"

"Where is he staying, Fedo?" Alessandro asked.

"Mestre," Federico said. "He's staying in Mestre."

"Thanks," Alessandro said. "Let's go, Partner."

120

3. *Palazzo Palladio*
On the Grand Canal

"The men were hilarious," Alessandro laughed. "Did you notice? They couldn't take their eyes off you. Old men, young men. The women, too. I think they were a bit, how we say in Italian, *Erano invidioso*. They were envious."

The night's activities at The Gritti Palace at the *Campo Santa Maria del Giglio* on the Grand Canal would be reported in the newspapers and magazines as the highlight of the city's social calendar. Guests of the Mayor included government officials, Army and Air Force generals and Navy admirals, from both the Italian and NATO military, diplomats from a dozen countries, and the city's most distinguished citizens, along with a few of the most recognizable entertainers. And, of course, the ubiquitous *paparazzi* with their cameras.

"Maybe it was this gorgeous diamond necklace they were all looking at," she said. "I don't think I've ever seen such a beautiful necklace. Maybe in the window at Tiffany's. Thank you for lending it to me for the night. And don't let me forget to return it to you. I'm a New York public servant. I'm not allowed to accept gifts, especially not such a valuable piece of jewelry."

"It wasn't the necklace," he said, taking her hand.

"Maybe they envied my escort," she said. "After all, the magazines say you're Italy's most eligible bachelor. So maybe the women were thinking, who is this stranger who has come to Venice from – who knows where? – to capture the heart of the great Alessandro, Viscount Palladio?"

Alessandro laughed. "I can only imagine what those men were thinking to themselves. Maybe their capacity for thought had escaped them. I don't blame them, my dear. You enchanted them – and me. I admit, I am still under your spell. Whatever gods there may be, my dear Gabriela. I thank them that you came into my life."

He took her hand to his lips and to his cheek. "And I thank your martial arts teachers for the way you handled yourself at the Ghetto! You did it, Partner. You were confident you would catch this monster, and you did it. You got him. Although, I must say, you had me on pins and needles, putting yourself in danger like that."

They had just climbed out of Alessandro's thirty-seven-foot Riva powerboat onto the steps leading into the ground floor of the house. They walked up the steps to the library. She was still feeling the exhilaration of the night and perhaps the lingering effects of a little too much *Prosecco*.

It was a grand celebration, with music and dancing, with food and entertainment. Serial killer captured in the *Museo Ebraica*. Case closed. Mission accomplished, on time and under budget! Tonight, the Mayor presented her with a huge elegant certificate, *Cittadina onoraria di Venezia*, Honorary Citizen of Venice, with the seal of the city embossed in gold leaf. And the president of the Venice Jewish community presented her with a medal and certificate of appreciation in the form of a scroll with hand drawn calligraphy and illuminated by illustrations representing the history of the Jewish presence in the city. She knew she was expected back in New York now that her mission had been completed, but not tonight. Not this night.

"He could have killed you," Sandro said, kneeling on the big man's back. He held him in a tight hammerlock and snapped the handcuffs around his wrists. "I don't ever want to see you play the decoy like that again. I was ready to jump out the moment I saw him coming through the door."

Gabriela knew what she was doing. Or, at least, she *thought* she knew. Seated in the synagogue above the Jewish Museum, her plan was to act the part of a shy young Jewish woman at prayer, expecting that he might approach her quietly from behind. After all, that was his *modus operandi*.

What she hadn't anticipated was the *speed* of the attack. She had been looking around in all directions and thought she was aware of her surroundings. No sooner had she turned her eyes back toward the front of the synagogue than he attacked her from the aisle on her right side. He grabbed her by the neck and started to strangle her.

"No more Jew babies for you, bitch!" the attacker hissed in her ear as he tightened his big hands around her neck. Her training kicked in immediately. She swiveled around in her seat to her left and brought her right foot over her left shoulder into the man's face. It was a move she had taught at the 92nd Street Y and had practiced a hundred times. Now facing her attacker, she brought both arms up and clapped her hands hard against his ears. Just as he loosened his grip on her neck, she head-butted him, smashing his nose.

By the time Alessandro came running out of his hiding place behind the heavy drape at the back wall, Gabriela had the attacker on the floor. His nose was broken and bleeding.

"He took me by surprise," she said. "For a big man, he was fast. I thought I was ready, but he came at me like a bolt of lightning. Boy, was he fast!'"

"Not fast enough for my partner," Alessandro said. "You were incredible. I bet he never knew what hit him. You got him."

"I was sent here to stop this maniac," she said. "He was too predictable. The only thing that bothered me was the sixth victim. I knew he had to kill six, but there are only five synagogues in Venice."

"But you figured it out, like a professional," Alessandro said. "You have the makings to be a fine detective, ADA Gabriela Sofia Nadal-Martin."

"The Museum," Gabriela said. "The fifth victim was to be upstairs in the synagogue. We knew that. But the sixth? It could only be downstairs, in the Museum. Probably the young woman at the front door. It would have been an ironic victory for him, killing the woman charged with security for the Museum and for the synagogue. We saved two lives tonight."

"It was smart to wear the plastic neck brace under your scarf," Sandro said. "And he really was a big man. Your profile was right on target. But you handled him like you have a black belt."

"I *do* have a black belt," she said. "Remember, I told you. And I've been teaching women how to defend themselves against this kind of attack."

"Ah, yes, I do remember," he said, "and as I recall, you cautioned me not to try any monkey business."

"Or words to that effect," she said. "Now let's get this lunatic to the cells."

It had been a risky plan. Any mistake could be lethal. They knew the killer was a big man, and ruthless. Alessandro had expressed his concern for Gabriela's safety, but she managed to pull it off perfectly. She was a good prosecutor, but she turned out to be a first-rate under-cover cop, as well. Still, her heart was throbbing as if she had just completed one of her one-hour classes in self-defense at the 92nd Street Y.

Three blue and white *polizia* boats had arrived in *Le rio di Ghetto Nuovo*, the small canal outside the *Museo Ebraica*. Six young *Carabinieri* officers jumped from the boats and ran through the Museum and up the stairs to the synagogue. They tied the killer's arms and legs with nylon ropes and dragged him up the aisle, out the door, and down the stairs to the ground floor. Case closed.

Almost closed. What remained was to discover who this monster is and what motivated him. Fingerprints and contacts with the American FBI revealed the answers. His name is Corwin Schmidt from rural Coeur d'Alene, Idaho, and he's known to be a member of the Aryan Nations, a white supremacist hate group.

Members of the Aryan Nations organization have been active in committing hate crimes against African Americans, Hispanics, Muslims, and Jews. Schmidt has a record of arrests in Idaho for domestic abuse and vandalism. Elders of the Church of Jesus Christ of Latter-day Saints excommunicated Corwin Schmidt six years ago. Since that time, he's become a member of the American Nazi Party, with the mission of killing young Jewish women, women who might give birth to Jewish babies.

A search of Schmidt's apartment in Mestre just north of the city revealed that he was already planning his next killing spree in Tel Aviv. He had detailed maps of the city showing streets and points of interest. He had located six synagogues in the city that would show the pattern of the six-pointed Star of David. He marked them on one of the maps and connected them, showing the pattern. With the hundreds of synagogues in Tel Aviv, selecting six in the pattern was a much easier task than he had in Venice.

Safely back in the library of the *Palazzo Palladio*, Gabriela said, "In America, we have a custom. A nice, time-honored custom."

"Yes," he said, "and what custom would that be? An American custom? You know we have customs here, too."

"Well," she said, "in America, when a boy brings a girl to her home after a date, he tries to give her a good night kiss. If it's a good date, she lets him kiss her. If it hasn't been a good night, she may shake his hand. But no kiss. Especially on the first date. But a good date, she puckers up for a kiss."

"Was this a date?" he asked.

"Well, let's evaluate the evidence. First, you asked me to accompany you to a celebration and a dinner, and we danced to romantic music."

"You dance very well," he said.

"Well, you know, I am Nuyorican, after all!"

"And second?" he asked.

"Second, you gave me this lovely little black dress from your sister's wardrobe and this diamond necklace and these diamond earrings."

"And third?"

126

"Third, you drove me in your beautiful boat to the Gritti Palace, where the Mayor made me an honorary citizen and the Jewish community gave me a medal."

"Well deserved," he said.

"Fourth, you danced with me all night."

"Much to the chagrin of the other men," he said.

"Fifth, last but not least, you brought me home safely to my door. It would seem the evidence is clear. I think that qualifies as a date."

"Well, given the overwhelming evidence presented in this case, and in the light of your nice, time-honored custom, I suppose I should try to give you a good night kiss. Was this a *good* date?"

"Inspector Colonel Signor, this was the best date of my life."

He put his hand on her cheek and touched his lips to hers. She put her hand around his neck and leaned in to press her lips to his.

"This was the best date for me, as well, my dear *Signorina* Gabriella Sofia Nadal-Martin. And not just because of the fun of seeing the expressions of those at the party. You made me feel young tonight. Thank you for that."

"I suppose I should take off this valuable diamond necklace," she whispered. "It would be a shame if it were to be lost. Will you undo the clasp? *Signore?*"

He leaned over her shoulder, undid the clasp, and removed the necklace. He placed it on the coffee table in front of the leather sofa.

"My dear, those diamonds have been in our family for many generations, but never have they adorned such a lovely neck."

127

She smiled and kissed him again. "And the zipper?" she whispered. "Would you be so kind as to help with the zipper?"

Again, he reached around her and slowly drew down the zipper from her neck to her waist.

She shrugged off the shoulders of the dress and it fell to the floor. Alessandro had not paid much attention to the lithe figure of his partner until he saw her that evening in the little black dress. Now that the dress was down at her ankles, he was struck by the stunning beauty of the figure of this young woman.

"You have no top," he observed.

"Can't be bothered," she said. "Are you embarrassed?" she asked.

"Not at all. I must say, Gabriella Sofia Nadal-Martin, you are surely the most beautiful woman in all Venice, no, in all Italy, no, in all the world."

"Well, then, you won't mind carrying me up the stairs?"

"It will be my privilege, *Signorina*, to carry you up to your room."

"Not to *my* room, Silly."

"She did a good job over there," the Governor said. "When is she coming home? I want to have a celebration. Mission accomplished. I want to give her a medal. And a promotion. That young lady has a bright future. Maybe District Attorney. Or Attorney General in a few years."

"She's not coming home, Governor," his secretary said.

"What do you mean, she's not coming home? Of course, she's coming home. She did what we sent her to do. She got her man. She isn't sick, is she? Or hurt?"

"Nothing like that, Governor. She's going to get married over there."

"Married? Over there? Who's she getting married to? Anybody we know."

"To an old friend of yours. Someone she met in Venice. I believe you know the man. A police officer."

"Ah, well, that would be Sandro. Alessandro Palladio, my Oxford rugby team mate," the Governor said. "I guess I'll take credit for the match between Gabriela and Sandro. But you know, Venice is a very romantic place."

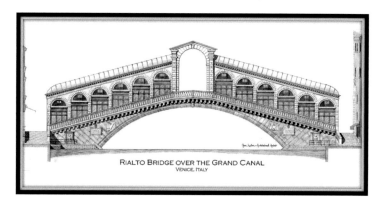

RIALTO BRIDGE OVER THE GRAND CANAL
VENICE, ITALY

The Four Seasons, by Antonio Vivaldi (1678-1741)

Vivaldi's arrangement of *The Four Seasons* is as follows:

- Concerto No. 1 in E major, Op. 8, RV 269, "Spring" (*La primavera*)
    1. Allegro (in E major)
    2. Largo e pianissimo sempre (in C♯ minor)
    3. Allegro pastorale (in E major)
- Concerto No. 2 in G minor, Op. 8, RV 315, "Summer" (*L'estate*)
    1. Allegro non molto (in G minor)
    2. Adagio e piano - Presto e forte (in G minor)
    3. Presto (in G minor)
- Concerto No. 3 in F major, Op. 8, RV 293, "Autumn" (*L'autunno*)
    1. Allegro (in F major)
    2. Adagio molto (in D minor)
    3. Allegro (in F major)
- Concerto No. 4 in F minor, Op. 8, RV 297, "Winter" (*L'inverno*)
    1. Allegro non molto (in F minor)
    2. Largo (in E♭ major)
    3. Allegro (in F minor)

https://en.wikipedia.org/wiki/The_Four_Seasons_ (Vivaldi)

The Four Seasons Sonnets

Spring

Allegro
Spring has arrived with joy
Welcomed by the birds with happy songs,
And the brooks, amidst gentle breezes,
Murmur sweetly as they flow.
The sky is caped in black, and
Thunder and lightning herald a storm
When they fall silent, the birds
Take up again their delightful songs.

Largo e pianissimo sempre
And in the pleasant, blossom-filled meadow,
To the gentle murmur of leaves and plants,
The goatherd sleeps, his faithful dog beside him.

Allegro pastorale
To the merry sounds of a rustic bagpipe,
Nymphs and shepherds dance in their beloved spot
When Spring appears in splendor.

Summer

Allegro non molto

Under the merciless sun of the season
Languishes man and flock, the pine tree burns.
The cuckoo begins to sing and at once
Join in the turtledove and the goldfinch.
A gentle breeze blows, but Boreas
Is roused to combat suddenly with his neighbour,
And the shepherd weeps because overhead
Hangs the fearsome storm, and his destiny.

Adagio e piano

His tired limbs are robbed of rest
By his fear of the lightning and the frightful thunder
And by the flies and hornets in furious swarms.

Presto

Alas, his fears come true:
There is thunder and lightning in the heavens
And the hail cuts down the tall ears of grain.
Autumn (Concerto No. 3 in F Major)

Autumn

Allegro
The peasant celebrates with dancing and singing
The pleasure of the rich harvest,
And full of the liquor of Bacchus
They end their merrymaking with a sleep.

Adagio molto
All are made to leave off dancing and singing
By the air which, now mild, gives pleasure
And by the season, which invites many
To find their pleasure in a sweet sleep.

Allegro
The hunters set out at dawn, off to the hunt,
With horns and guns and dogs they venture out.
The beast flees and they are close on its trail.
Already terrified and wearied by the great noise
Of the guns and dogs, and wounded as well
It tries feebly to escape, but is bested and dies.

———————————————

Winter

Allegro non molto

Frozen and shivering in the icy snow,
In the severe blasts of a terrible wind
To run stamping one's feet each moment,
One's teeth chattering through the cold.

Largo

To spend quiet and happy times by the fire
While outside the rain soaks everyone.

Allegro

To walk on the ice with tentative steps,
Going carefully for fear of falling.
To go in haste, slide, and fall down to the ground,
To go again on the ice and run,
In case the ice cracks and opens.
To hear leaving their iron-gated house Sirocco,
Boreas, and all the winds in battle—
This is winter, but it brings joy.

Antonio Vivaldi

The Layout of Venice

Acknowledgements

Grazie molto to the most hospitable staff at the Hotel Rialto. Anna, "our mighty Housekeeper"; Front Desk Staff: Mauro, Gabriele, Marco, and Gianni; and Breakfast Staff: Mara, Luminita, Rachele, Chiara B., and Chiara F. You made our three weeks stay pleasant and productive. And memorable. *Noi non ti dimenticherò mai.*

To the many people of Venice who made us feel at home, *Grazie a tutti voi!*

The author gratefully acknowledges the wisdom shared by Rabbi David Ross Senter of Temple Israel in Portsmouth, New Hampshire.

This collection of short stories could not have seen the light of day without the assistance of my wife and life partner, Danna Hilary Vance Raupp. *Un milione di grazie, il mio amore!*

Thanks to Gina Troisi (http://gina-troisi.com/), my colleague at Great Bay Community College in Portsmouth, New Hampshire. Her commentaries helped to make these stories more engaging for our dear readers.

Sonnet translation by Betsy Schwarm.
https://www.britannica.com/topic/The-Four-Seasons-by-Vivaldi
Signature from Wikipedia Commons.

Front cover: Filip Mihail, *Rialto Bridge,* by permission of the artist. See his work at
https://www.saatchiart.com/art/Painting-Rialto-Bridge/163085/1419968/view

On the Steps of the Rialto Bridge: drawing adapted from *http://www.123rf.com/clipart-vector/the_rialto_bridge.html*

Il Pescheria, The Fish Market:
http://resizeandsave.online/openphoto.php?img=http://www.artetmer.com/uploads/images/oeuvres/peche/Haquette1.jpg

The Unicorn in Giardini Papadopoli: Image adapted from *http://www.labcoloring.com/photos-of-unicorn-coloring-pages/winged-unicorn-coloring-pages-for-kids-3/*

Piazza San Marco:
http://www.karmatoons.com/doodles/doodles15.htm

Death Comes to Burano: Photograph from Martina Vidal Venezia with permission. See www.martinavidal.com.

Pelleteria Tedeschi: Shears.
https://www.knifecenter.com/item/ON4004/Ontario-Kitchen-Shears-3-inch-Carbon-Steel-Blades

Alberoni Beach, Lido di Venezia: Drawing by Rene Bouet-Williaumez. *Alla vita!* To life!
http://keywordsuggest.org/gallery/592216.html

Jet aircraft: *clipart-library.com*

Murano:https://giftsandcollectiblesgalore.wordpress.com/2013/01/05/murano-decorative-art-the-history/

Farewell, My Hero *mightymac.org/europe12/12europe10.htm*

A Police Story:

1. *Palazzo Cavalli. Alamy.com*

2. The Venice Jazz Club: Trumpet player:
https://www.pinterest.com/pin/392024342535170796/

3. *Palazzo Palladio:* Grand Canal and Rialto Bridge:
Rialto Bridge over the Grand Canal by Gene Nelson.
http://fineartamerica.com/featured/rialto-bridge-venice-gene-nelson.html

The Layout of Venice:
http://www.reidsitaly.com/destinations/veneto/venice/planning/venice_layout.html

The Author

Edward Raupp - soldier, business executive, educator. As a Peace Corps Volunteer in the former Soviet Republic of Georgia from 2003 to 2006, he was a member of the Faculty of English Language and Literature at Gori State University. He has taught English, economics, and other courses in Georgia, Tanzania, and the United States.

He earned a BS from Carnegie Mellon University; MBA from the Wharton School of the University of Pennsylvania; MA in English Language and Literature from the University of Minnesota; and PhD in Economics from The University of Georgia in Tbilisi. He studied at Christ Church, Oxford, and graduated with distinction from the Army Command and General Staff College and the United States Naval War College. He retired from the Army as a colonel in 1978.

Dr. Raupp has been teaching for over twenty-five years. He chaired the Department of Business and Economics at Waldorf College (now Waldorf University) in Forest City, Iowa, for seven years. During that time, he founded the Waldorf Dar es Salaam branch campus in Tanzania (now TUDARCO) and served as its Dean and Chief Academic Officer, and developed and taught economics, developing and transitional nations, statistics, and other courses. He co-founded Friends of Africa Education to expand capacity and improve access to education in Tanzania. After Peace Corps, he was Chancellor of The University of Georgia, Tbilisi, and is its Emeritus Distinguished Professor.

He is married to the former Danna Hilary Vance. They teach economics courses as a team at Great Bay Community College in Portsmouth, New Hampshire.

Made in the USA
Middletown, DE
19 December 2020